Marti and Anna
Out of Cuba

Colado

Praise for Marti and Anna: Out of Cuba

"A deeply personal and multicultural story that tugs at your heart. You will love it."
- Dr. Milton E. Polsky, former professor at CUNY, and co-author with Warren Wyss of the mystery-history novel,
Shadows on Bleecker Street

"[Colado] does an excellent job of creating full characters for Anna, Jimmy, Marti, and Alfredo. Through revealing their backgrounds, as well as showing their personalities, the reader understands why they became who they are. Both Anna and Marti confronted extremely difficult situations when they were young, wounds they carried with them their entire lives and ones that have shaped them. She creates them objectively and that's no small feat."
- Martine Bellen, poet, editor, and librettist.
  Author of *This Amazing Cage of Light*

"Rich and evocative, Colado's Cuban-American family memoir brings characters and time periods to life with sensitivity and humor."
- Kohenet Ellie Barbarash, writer and reviewer

"Your novel shows much imagination"
- Susan Metz writer and independent researcher

For information regarding permission,
contact us at our website:
www.coladowrites.com

ISBN: 978-0-9967402-0-3

Library of Congress Number: 2015951329

Published by: R.E. Phillips, Tampa, Florida

Printed in the United States of America

Printed September 2015

Marti & Anna: Out of Cuba

DEDICATION

Dedicated to my mother Marta and Grandmother Anna. Their intelligence, courage, and struggles continue to be an inspiration to the family.

Marti and Anna
Out of Cuba

Colado

CONTENTS

Colado

ACKNOWLEDGMENTS

I want to thank Russ Phillips for his creative photographic genius in taking the photos and from them designing the book cover. Also for his advice in creating the novel's structure. My sincere appreciation to Miguel Alberto Hamond, who painstakingly reproduced the elderly photos within the novel. I wish to thank Martine Bellen and Lina Carmona for their editing work.
To Milton Polsky, author of over twenty books including his latest (co-authored), "Shadows On Bleecker Street." Milton, you painstakingly whittled my manuscript into a sturdy novel. Thank you for your kindness.
To you my dear husband Eugene, I appreciate your encouragement and suggestions.

Colado

PROLOGUE

He raised his voice so loud everyone at the nearby tables turned.
"I still can't believe that Aunt Anna is really my grandmother! Why didn't you tell me before!"

"Because I thought you knew!" Norma said in a growling low voice, embarrassed by her brother airing family business in public. Norma's brother Alfredo Jr., even at fifty-five, was still clueless about many things. Family things, as we all are, she supposed. He always had been a solitary type, spending free time alone, hunting or fishing.

Now Alfredo, Jr. lowered his voice in the crowded restaurant.

"You should've told me, Norma."

"I didn't mention it because I told you, thought you knew. Lighten up, Alfredo" Norma started to smile.

"Don't be funny like Papa was. This is serious." Alfredo replied.

No matter how she explained, Norma's brother remained angry.

This is the story of Norma's grandmother, Anna and mother, Marti and their family. It is a story created from history, family memories, and the imagination like a distaff which holds images. Some stories lie inside shells, not discussed because of pride, fear, guilt, shame, and customs. The shells have been torn opened; the past is in the present...

In the late 1940s Marti watched the skies darken around velvety gray clouds, as two of her three children climbed onto tree limbs whose branches bent to the ground and shook their clinging bodies. Alfredo Jr. and Norma rode the trees like cowboys on mounts. Gusts swept the tree branches into rhythmic waves. The cats sensed the weather change and dashed into the cellar of the lemon-colored farmhouse. Raindrops announced the approaching torrent, and the children ran into the house.

So predictable their lives had been, resembling the change of seasons. The routines and people mingled, threads interwoven into a fabric of sturdy material. Life's later experiences would fray the fabric, like ripping strands of tree roots. Yet brilliant streaks of similar threads remained visible, where warm memories and reticent stories were pulled apart and examined.

Marti's childhood had been the opposite, unpredictable. At thirteen, she was taken out of her Cuban boarding school to be brought to North America by her mother, later marrying a man from a large family who spent weeks away recuperating from a chronic illness. Hers was a dream of an only child, but still looming was the threat of loss she learned when young.

Marti's glimmering memories of her aunt/mother Anna (Juana was her given name) were ingrained with the odor of the ink as she turned newspaper pages; the crackling of aged water pipes; and the frightening sight of live lobsters clawing frantically at the inside of the metal pot after being plunged into boiling water. How could she forget how those cooked, hacked lobsters were poured over a thick tomato sauce, then over steaming cornmeal?

Marti also remembered that Anna wore narrow multicolored scarves tied around her frizzy hair. Dangling robin egg-blue wooden balls or other earrings popped out from underneath her scarves, punctuating animated discussions where hands and heads flew all around. Her broken English would draw laughs when she exclaimed, "Me speak good English!" Her shapely five-foot-eight frame was always highlighted in bright-flowered polyester dresses, stockings rolled into garters, and stylish ankle-hugging shoes.

Marti recalled, too, the plastic-covered inaugural photo hanging on the wall of President Reagan, his smiling wife wearing a mushroom-like cap. That photo would elicit squints from Marti's daughter, who blossomed in the'70's hippie antiwar atmosphere. Years later, her children came to love visiting Anna and exploring the thin metal cans filled with flakey, bent Cuban crackers and chewing the salty cheese-laden corkscrew snacks. Their mother would not allow such treats at home because they were "unhealthy."

Before the Cross Bronx Expressway cleaved the area back in the early 1940s, Anna's apartment was within a brick house on a tree-lined block next to an empty lot filled with wild flowers. She had lived with her husband in many apartments, once even owning Manhattan brownstones. They were saving money to buy a two-family house in this quieter Bronx, a suburb, as Anna called it, of her beloved Manhattan.

Norma, then four, loved to run among the surrounding wildflowers when visiting Anna's house. "No, you cannot go out. It is dangerous!" Anna cautioned during one such visit after the child peeked out from the front door.

"I'll come right back," Norma later whispered to her older brother Alfredo Jr. as she darted out the door and up the concrete walkway toward the beckoning flowers. She was anxious to join ten-year-old Leslie, the daughter of Mercedes, Anna's upstairs neighbor and Norma's older sister Maria. Hopscotch, called *"pon"* in Cuba, was their favorite game.

"¿Dónde tu va? Where are you going?" Leslie demanded, taking hold of her little friend's hand.

In response, Norma bit Leslie's upper arm, leaving a clear set of front teeth marks. Leslie pushed her and ran upstairs, crying, "Mama, she attacked me!"

When surrounded by adults, Norma denied this happened but the teeth marks, plainly visible, were indisputable evidence. Marti apologized and dragged her weeping daughter down the path lined with wildflowers and into Anna's apartment.

Anna grabbed Norma as Marti began to shake and chase her daughter around the kitchen.

"Negrita, it is better not to punish her. Let her play outside for a while," said Anna, hugging the child, who dissolved into her apron like wet snowflakes.

"But, Anna, she just does not listen," Marti replied angrily.

"You need more patience with her," Anna snapped back.

"You don't live with a sick husband and three children!"

Marti drew in a heavy breath. She knew Anna's stone-face said: *I warned you not to marry a sick man.*

They remained silent until Anna walked Marti and the children to the car for their two-hour drive back upstate. Anna felt sorry for what she had said. It was best to use prudence. Marti, in turn, knew she shouldn't be upset by anything her opinionated mother said. She now lived far enough away that she didn't have to deal with her regularly. *Anna did me a favor by sending me to boarding school,* she reasoned. *It made me more independent.* But deep inside her soul, the threads binding her emotionally to Anna would not go away.

As she drove toward the bridge, the Bronx brick row houses changed into the apartment buildings of Upper Manhattan. She

4

slowed down as the setting sun's rays pierced her eyes. A car behind her honked incessantly, and then sped around her at an intersection, passing a red pulsating traffic signal.

"To hell with you!" she yelled, making sure the sleeping children in the back seat were okay. In reality, Maria pretended sleeping to avoid her mother's anger. Driving was just one of the challenges Marti had overcome, even though she kept under the posted speed limits. Passing the Palisades' cliffs, Marti's feelings about her mother softened: *Anna, even with all her moral faults, tried to be on my side since I arrived from Cuba.* She glanced at her own children, understanding that child rearing was stressful. "A pity we were separated for so many years," Marti said out loud. But she silently thanked God for the Oblate Sisters, who through those troublesome years taught her what was right.

Colado

1 ANNA
1895 - 1919

Anna would ride a horse to school on paths bordered by lank tobacco plants. She always carried a thinly sliced pork sandwich. Her trips to school were calming, solitary times when nothing was asked of her. But once she began menstruating, her father told her she could no longer attend.

"It is dangerous to travel alone."

"Why?" Anna's independent spirit burst open like a grape-like squeezed quenepa.

"It is too dangerous for you to ride alone. That's it!"

"But I always ride alone to school."

"You are a young lady now, Juana," he explained, rubbing dirt from his palm, secure in the knowledge that as his daughter, she must obey.

"If I can not go to school or see my friends, I do not want to be a young lady!" Anna could not hold back her tears.

"You do not talk back to me! Your mother needs you at home to care for your brother and sisters." He began to remove his belt, but the sight of her defiant, angry face stopped him.

"This behavior will not be allowed in my house!" His growl punctured the air. "Juana, your mother is expecting again," he added, watching her face soften as he had predicted it would. "Who will bring in the charcoal, clean rice, carry plantains, and kill the chickens for dinner? I must attend to the harvest. You understand?"

"No!" she shouted, running into the tobacco field toward a clump of gray palms, their branches reaching out to console her. Her father strode over to the wooden house, shutters open to allow the breeze to sweep away heat. He cursed her brash disrespect, knowing that his house for Juana was Pluto's Hades.

Anna, born in 1895, lived in the Western Province of Pinar del Rio in the valley of Consolación del Sur. Viscid tobacco plants surrounded her wooden house, topped by intertwining palm branches. This roof went back to the Amerindian *bohios*. In this house lived the Collados. A winding dirt road, crisscrossed by horse and cart tracks, connected other simple houses in an area surrounded by dense vegetation, and mats of green warmth, on which the sun's rays glistened after the hurried rains subsided.

The area was formed by undersea mountain peaks, which emerged as the earth's plates shifted over fifty to seventy million years ago, volcanic eruptions piercing the earth. During quieter eras, the seas covered parts of the island depositing decayed marine animals, sand, and limestone. Amerindians populated the South American mainland ten thousand years before the birth of Christ. Some found their way into Cuba, thinking that they were not living on "islands," but on "land with an abundance of water," some water being drinkable.

Anna's father, like his father before him, was a *veguero* or small tobacco farmer. He later supervised railroad workers in the first rail system built in Latin America between 1837 and 1838. Her grandfather, the father of six sons, would tell many stirring stories about the old days.

"In the 1700s my father made more money selling tobacco to the English and French sailors rather than to the Spaniards who controlled with terror and decrees since the early 1500s," he would say, waving a cigar at the side of his Amerindian-carved mouth.

Those "sailors" were pirates Anna later found out.

"The sailors hide their ships inside small keys. Cubans sold them tobacco, sugar, molasses, cigars, and hides."

"Was that dangerous?" gasped an amazed Anna. Her imagination was swelling like rising Cuban bread.

"Yes, they could jail him, so he traveled on foot to the shore with the supplies in straw bags," her grandfather explained, expelling a cumulus-shaped cloud of smoke.

"Later, viceroys passed laws to control what could be sold. He couldn't even sell extras. They wanted him to produce less. Taxes were increased. He protested and joined a march into the capital. They arrested the leaders and executed them. A group of them decided to sell the land."

Anna's grandmother handed her husband a sweetened cup of black coffee and boiled milk. He blew on it, swirling the curdled milk to one side of the cup. Anna's grandfather said, "Many went to Pinar del Rio along the Cuyaguateje River. It was a moneymaking choice because this area, Consolación, grows even better tobacco.

9

He got up from the table to hoe in between tobacco plants. Anna followed him.

Later, sitting by the river eating the lunch Anna had carried to her bass-fishing grandfather, they were startled by new sounds. Crossing a shallow part of the river they saw a couple with regal postures. Clearly, they were landowners. They wore crown-like straw hats, loose cotton shirts, matching rolled-up pants, and sandals. And they carried machetes over their shoulders.

"Buenos días," the couple chimed in. Her grandfather remarked how lucky they were to have found the river low today, their crossing made easy.

"There is another river, the Ariguanabo, named after the peoples who lived here thousands of years ago. It starts and ends in Pinar del Río. It is fed by several springs originating from the tops of faraway mountains. Indians used the river to haul goods between villages. They say its water has healing properties, but the river can be dangerous as heavy rains and the wind make the currents strong. In the 1600s, some Cubans were joined by Mexican loggers, and they worked on the river together."

"Where is Mexico?"

"A country to the west of Cuba."

He continued while eager-to-hear Anna ate her boiled plantain.

"The boat overturned and the three Mexicans, all brothers, fell into the river and drowned. The rest could swim. A fourth brother spent two years diving down to the bottom of the water to carve a cross on a stone. The cross is visible when the river is low. Anna remained quiet, listening to the man whom she admired. Yes, in her heart, he had grown to replace her dictatorial father.

Anna did quit school to help her mother, then for several years picked dirt from rice grains, preparing chicken and earth vegetable stews. Her favorite chore was riding to town to buy supplies and meeting the friends she missed from school. Her father had accepted a position with the railroad company and was gone, supervising crews for weeks at a time. She regretted when he did return and hoped his short visits home would keep him from noticing what her mother already knew.

It was only a matter of time before he actually saw her weight gain. One day he was watching her pump water from the well and her baggy blouse lifted. When she came into the house, Anna's father slapped her so hard she fell against the bureau, shattering a mirror. When he asked about their daughter's growing lower abdomen, his wife pretended to be surprised.

"Keep the child," Anna's mother had advised her bewildered daughter. "I will tell your father when the time comes." But he found out before the opportunity came up. Luckily, Anna's mother had spoken to Graciela her brother's wife about the matter. She helped Anna by providing shelter and a job away from home—as the nanny for the children of a captain in the Cuban army—following the birth of her daughter.

"I did not understand how it happened. I was young," Anna would later tell her granddaughter, Norma. But she could not bear to share the details of what transpired until many years had passed.

"My father, he hated me too much," Anna said but spoke lovingly of her siblings, especially her younger brother.

Anna cherished the photo of her brother wearing his Cuban military uniform. His tan face stood out warmly from under a curved, banded hat. He was wearing puffy tan pants, stuffed loosely into knee-high boots. Epaulets guarded his shirt's shoulders, a sword jetting out smartly from his belt.

This is the same uniform the Capitan wore, Anna thought as she got up. She walked over to the stove to stir the rice as the water began to boil—then added salt and oil to the mushy consistency. She lowered the flame and placed a heavy lid on top of the cast-iron pot, trapping the steam that burst the rice grains like blossoms in spring.

The Capitan provided Anna with a salary, so she became independent of her controlling father. Her mother's only demand had been "Keep the baby. Bring it to me." And Anna had. The baby bonded with her grandmother. Aunt Graciela would bring Anna news of the family when she delivered money home for her daughter, Marti. Anna was pragmatic, quick to speak her mind (right or wrong), and outgoing. She loved to gossip with friends, so relieved to live in a household that was far away from her father's rage and her daughter, whom---in her heart---she blamed for her exile from home.

Anna found it easy to take charge of the Capitan's three children. Armando was her favorite because he shared family secrets with her. Anna soon learned that the nervous, helpless the Capitan's wife, Doña Alicia, had been fragile from childhood on. This was because her mother had emotionally detached from her when she learned of her husband's second family with a *mulata* who lived in a nearby town. Armando's mother nearly fainted the time Armando fell off the balcony and ran to her with his cracked twiglike wrist. Anna wrapped a towel around his arm, waved a passing carriage, and instructed the driver how to travel to the doctor's house. So upsetting was Alicia's crying, that along with the driver's hands, the reins and attached martingale quivered.

Chubby Doña Alicia fanned her face in waves like flapping butterfly wings. "La mestiza quickly cared for Armando."

"Yes, and the children like her," said the thin, Cuban-born

captain, who read all he could find about ships and sea travel. He bent over his mahogany desk, light from the stained glass shining on it. He was pleased by how quickly Anna adapted to their lifestyle.

What thrilled sixteen-year-old Anna most was not the six-room, two-story, coral limestone house adorned with columns around the curved porch, the deep rust-colored tile floors and roof--- or her own room. Nor was it the maid who washed her clothes, or the meals prepared by the cook. No, it was the exciting opportunity to visit the friends she had been forbidden to see by her stern father.

Anna was elated to travel with the Capitan's family, which included visits to his parents in Havana. The Capitan's parents lived in an architecturally Mudejar-influenced house of ribbed ceilings and intricate window grillwork. She was overjoyed walking on the carriage-filled streets, among elegantly dressed city women. One year later, the family visited the Doña's family in Spain. This journey the Capitan particularly loved, as he spent most of the weeks by the side of sailors. From Spain, they visited Morocco. Two years later, they traveled to New York City, Anna attracted to it like a butterfly to a flower's nectar. She had not understood the source of the family's wealth that had paid for these trips or the relationship of their family's fortune to the struggles against Spanish domination. The Capitan's ancestors had amassed wealth from large tracts of land and from the Amerindians who worked for them.

In the 1600s, Yoruban and Bantu region slaves replaced the destroyed or runaway natives. During the years that sugar, molasses, wood, and people were traded, Chinese men added to the labor force. Slavery was abolished after the Ten Years War in 1878 when slaves joined the Spanish plantation owners and others who abhorred slavery. The insurrections continued until the end of the eighteenth century. However, Spaniards--- mostly poverty stricken--- continued to pour into Cuba, even during these periods of political unrest. These Spaniards joined the Cuban Creole population as domestics, military men, small farmers, business owners, or craftsmen.

Anna would remember many years later the Galician-born member of her family saying on how the wealthy people in Spain had a servant for every room. He recalled watching women wash their clothes in a river while the sunset cast safflower rays on them—a gallant pseudo-romantic scene like those in Benito Pérez Galdós's novels. Tensions continued in Cuba when better positions were held for Spaniards born into certain families, as in the case of the Capitan.

Anna accepted her reality without questioning the politics behind it and blamed her parents for their lack of education. She grew to love the Capitan's children, whom she felt weren't such an emotional burden as was her daughter Marti.

Anna recounted stories of her grandfather to the children she helped raise. "The first Cubans gathered shellfish, wild fruit, ate yucca, hunted iguanas. Yes, imagine damming pools of water for storage of fish and green turtles for food," she shared with Armando.

Caves dotted the thick green landscape of Western Cuba. Inseparable Anna and Armando hiked during the evening, when cloudlike mist sent shivers through palms trees. During rains they constructed skeletal *bohios* of palm leaves. While in the area Anna sometimes visited her mother, and Armando played with her younger siblings. Tulia, her older sister, traded local gossip that Anna found uninteresting. She blamed Tulia for her pregnancy, but they did not speak about it. Tulia was too embarrassed, Anna too angry. She was a caterpillar who could not return to its chrysalis. So she set her family aside and moved forward on her journey.

When the Capitan was assigned to the Havana Province, closer to ports that facilitated family travel, Anna was eager to leave and travel out of the country. She wrote: *Mother, in Spain there are hills dotted with pink blooming flowers on almond trees whose barks are as dark as the dirt around them.*

In Morocco, the streets are lined with trees filled with oranges. It is like stepping into the Bible. The men wear jellabas, robes, and little caps. The women wear caftans and some wear veils after they marry.

Anna's mother hid the letters from her husband.

You know, Arab people lived in Spain for eight hundred years, and they would speak to me first in their language and then in Spanish. Anna laughed as she wrote, shaking her head, her earrings and bracelets shimmying.

Years later, she would relate the story to her boyfriend, Jimmy, who worked in the garment industry. "You dye fabric in big tanks. But in Morocco they dye in holes ... yes, holes!" She paused for him to follow the process.

"Dyeing of fabric in Morocco is done in between stone buildings. There are many holes in the ground, like giant crab holes, lined with tile where the dye is poured. Men mix the wool yarn with poles. I saw yarns in purples and reds hanging on outside wooden drying racks."

Jimmy followed her along, laughing a bit. "We dye fabric and yarn and dry them in huge vats here in New York. You know, Mayor La Guardia does not permit holes or stains in alleyways."

During one trip to New York City, Anna walked the streets, at times getting lost until she found a Spanish-speaking vendor who directed her to the hotel. Returning to Cuba, she vowed to come back to its many different people and plentiful boarding houses. Her mother smiled uneasily at Anna's wish to leave Cuba. Anna understood how much her mother needed her to care for her siblings and daughter during holidays. Five years had passed since she gave birth to Marti, and she noticed how thin her mother had become. She would tire easily and go into her room after the evening meal. Within six months, Anna was called back from Havana. Her mother had died from tuberculosis. A distraught Marti had to be pulled away from the bedside of her dead grandmother after repeated attempts to awaken her. Anna's father remarried and spent less time on his farm. In defiance of her father's wish, Marti was placed in a Havana boarding school closer to where Anna worked. He had wanted her sister to care for Marti.

Anna would bring her luminous spirit from Cuba to New York, the special place she loved. Her determination would be passed on to Marti who, despite her feelings of shame, succeeded in forming a family and life independent of Anna. Marti's daughters would also inherit their grandmother's unflinching determination. To be sure, their free spirit rattled cautious Marti.

In 1917, while scouring the Havana newspapers for a job in New York, Anna found an ad for an experienced nanny and rushed to finish the paperwork. Julio, her boyfriend at the time, was against the trip. "But you could meet me in New York," Anna insisted naively, thinking that he would follow her. By 1918, her papers were in order. She booked passage and found a reasonably priced boarding house in Manhattan.

When Anna arrived in New York, she asked Mrs. Conklin, the woman who placed the ad for a nanny and sponsored her trip, if she had "a room only for me to sleep in?" Her English was so broken that she had to repeat her words three times.

"Why, no, none of our staff sleep *here*," Mrs. Conklin finally answered, looking on in amazement as Anna, hearing her, stormed out the door with only *"Te veo."*

"Well, I never!" Mrs. Conklin snickered out loud.

Anna practically flew down the Manhattan streets, purchased the Spanish-language newspaper, and returned to the rooming house owned by a Puerto Rican family. She turned on her radio and began reading the want ads. Anna found factory work embroidering after the 1911 New York City Triangle Shirtwaist Factory fire, which killed 146 immigrant women. Working conditions had improved. By 1920, the International Ladies Garment Workers Union was formed. Anna learned to negotiate the trolley car system and get to work.

"Anna, you walk for blocks. What are you looking for?" asked Lola Perez, who also lived in the boarding house on West 93rd

Street. They were to become close friends.

"I watch people, Lola, smell the food in carts, and taste new foods like the Irish stew for fifteen cents today."

Soon, Anna met other single women from Central America and the Caribbean through her work. They formed a women's social club. With her natural skills, she was elected treasurer. They held dances and smiled demurely at the young men.

Lola, born in Puerto Rico, owned the popular beauty shop in their neighborhood. She was barely five feet, shapely, and she dressed fashionably, wearing all the changing styles she found in the many dog-eared magazines in her two-room beauty salon. It had one sink and four hair dryers. She bleached her brown hair blond, Mae West style, flattering her light complexion and gray eyes. She always checked her thick, deep red lipstick for stains after smoking a thin cigar from her Cuban boyfriend. Her tight, short skirts purposely showed her ample rear. Anna walked to the Roxy Theatre with Lola, who was showered by whistles. Her keen business mind liberated her during a time when most women stayed home, awaiting their husband's paycheck. She was born in Ponce and had moved to New York with her handsome, five-foot-eleven, dark-complexioned Cuban boyfriend. There, in addition to owning the beauty parlor, they started a travel business among the Latinos in East Harlem.

Lola suggested Anna visit an employment agency for a higher paying job. For one year Anna cared for Carlito, the four-year-old son of a Cuban UN diplomat who lived on East 88th Street. She played freely with Carlito like she did with her own siblings, all the while chatting in rapid-fire Spanish.

Years later, her granddaughter Norma would think of Anna when watching the Caribbean nannies rolling strollers with white babies on the Upper East Side of Manhattan, or while they watched them on park benches, busily whispering to one another as their charges slept. Norma wondered why Americans hired foreign nannies. Was it because their salaries were lower than American-born women, or because the perception that a foreign-born person could provide greater safety than an American born? Maybe it really was because they were less jaded, less angry at the wealthy for ignoring the lower classes. It could be because they were less likely to use drugs. Norma remembered the TV show *Upstairs, Downstairs*, where the Irish joined British household staff who had the same stuffy attitudes toward the Irish (as did their employers toward all of their staff). Perhaps that is why Anna later supported the Republicans.

Graciela's husband, a merchant marine, helped Anna find a

higher paying job. He heard chambermaids were being hired at the Commodore Hotel. *"¿Dónde está El Commodor* (living room)?" Anna asked Lola.

"No, El Commodore, Anna. I will take you there tomorrow. Your English is not very good."

"Me speak good English," Anna insisted.

"Mira, this is a palace, Lola," she said outside of the stately Beaux-Arts-style hotel, recently built over the East 42nd Street subway station. They entered through a front door to nods from the doorman, whose friendly smile greeted the girls immersed in chatter. At the desk, Lola pointed to Anna. "She came to work here."

"The entrance is left of the front door, down the end of the block," the full-of-himself but amused desk clerk replied. He leaned over the mahogany counter to watch the tall, foreign-looking one and the petite one wiggle away. Lola remembered how an agency worker's smile faded when Lola had applied for a job where she was asked whether or not that "sweet accent" was French. Her retort was, "No, from Puerto Rico."

"That is why you should save money and start your own business," Lola advised her friend.

During the interview Anna was quiet as a stone, allowing Lola to do all the talking.

"You understand what you are expected to do?" the lady asked in English, her eyes squarely on the lean, dark one.

"Yes," Anna finally said after Lola slipped behind the lady and vigorously nodded.

"Good. You will report here Monday at eight a.m. in full uniform. Here is the list of the attire to bring with you."

Anna pressed her uniform twice and carefully matched her stockings to her oxford deep-blue shoes. The hotel was even more ornate than those she had stayed in while traveling with the Spaniards. She saved all her tips to pay for her US immigration process. She would become a citizen.

2 MAN WITH THE FUNNY ACCENT
1920

"¿Quiere bailar?" inquired a man who spoke an odd kind of Spanish. "No," she replied, hoping the man who had earlier asked her to dance would do so again.

The man with the odd accent asked again, and she said no. She finally agreed after he persisted in such an even, gentlemanly way to sit down next to her. They talked for the rest of the night. Even though she usually took the trolley car he walked her home, twenty blocks. Jimmy, who was twenty-six-years-old, had been raised in Calabria, Southern Italy. His family had earmarked him to become a priest, but he had different plans. He fought in the Italian -North African conflict, and then emigrated to New York to escape his religious family, though now he wrote to them frequently.

Jimmy, a skilled fabric chemical dyer, had a thin five-foot-nine frame and wore suspenders to hold up his gray, neatly pressed pants. The trousers precisely touched his European-style brown, pointed leather shoes with tiny holes dotting the front tops. He made sure to keep them shiny at all times. He wore tan or gray fedoras with black bands or a flattened Italian cap in assorted plaids.

Jimmy's angular Mediterranean face, with his hawk-like glances, would soften into a sparrow's smile once he knew you, and he was no longer shy. Anna would look on intently as Jimmy tapped the top of his partially boiled eggs to make a hole large enough for him to tip the slippery contents into his mouth. He would set a bottle of rum on the table and play dominoes with friends. He sipped the rum from a small shot glass while chatting in an easy way, about politics, sports, and the day's events.

Please, Julio, be honest, will you ever come to New York? Anna wrote in her weekly letters to her boyfriend, despite his infrequent letters to her. *Marti will be sent for soon, and you know how she feels about you,* added Anna, hoping that guilt would prod him.

No, Anna, he finally wrote. By the time this reply arrived, Anna's sister, Tulia, had written that she had seen Julio on several occasions on the street with his old girlfriend. Anna tore up all his letters and cried, feeling betrayed once again. She kept Jimmy at a distance for nearly a year, still hoping Julio would join her in New York. Jimmy remained patient. Their long walks continued, and on one Anna heard about Jimmy's solo journey to New York City in search of adventure. Their relationship grew, with Anna picking up various Italian phrases along the way.

"Anna, how long have we known one another?" Jimmy asked, as they sat on a bench at the 110th Street entrance to Central Park, their favorite spot.

"Over a year. Why?"

He leaned over and kissed her cheek. "That's why. You know how fond I am of you."

"Yes, but I told you that I want to be careful before I marry. It was difficult, as you know, in Cuba. I worked away from home and learned to be independent. That is important to me… to be able to make my own decisions even if sometimes they have been the wrong ones…"

She did not want to let go of Julio, hoping he would have a change of heart.

"Alright, Anna, no commitments to marriage… but could we live together? Look what we'd save in rent. If we save money from our salaries, one day we could afford to buy a house."

Silence from both for several minutes. "I'm not ready, Jimmy."

He loved her outgoing nature, her carefree spirit, and sense of staunch independence. He had always been a reserved man. But he was patient. Jimmy began to visit her Saturday afternoons in her brightly decorated room filled with tassels and artificial flowers she made on one of her several jobs. They grew more and more to trust one another.

They decided to save for their first shared apartment together, which was around West 145th Street. Soon they found it financially rewarding to apartment-hop, move every year or so. This was because they received the first month free, a tactic landlords used to attract tenants. Anna combined what would have been that month's rent money and a portion of Jimmy's salary into a savings account.

"Marriage is not necessary until we know for sure. *Siete d'accordo?*"

"Sí," Anna said, with a little hug. They would wait to marry until 1934, a secret they kept from their friends.

They bought their first brownstone in Upper Manhattan and rented their downstairs rooms to pay the mortgage. They sold the building for a nice profit and purchased a larger building in the neighborhood. Their first and only child was a miscarriage. Anna had come home when she felt cramps that continued after Jimmy arrived from work. Suddenly she felt a stream of fluid ooze from her vagina. She stuffed a pad inside her new panties and laid down. Jimmy called the doctor, but before he had time to arrive Anna expelled a ten-week fetus. Appalled by its froglike still face, they wrapped the fetus in the bed sheet.

"It looks funny," she said to the doctor. Jimmy looked down at Anna's engagement ring that was dotted with small diamonds, which reminded him of dewdrops on a spider's web. Their gaze rested on the blood on her hand. She did not become pregnant again.

Soon Anna spoke about bringing to New York her thirteen-year-old "niece" Marti, who lived in a private girl's Catholic boarding school in Havana. Jimmy knew their new dream was of buying another building to rent out rooms. This would require Anna to work. So he naturally asked, "Do you want to take the responsibility of raising a child? Would you continue to work?"

"Of course, I would work. Marti will also work during the day and attend night school. She could help us earn money, while continuing her education."

"But she's only thirteen."

"We could say she is a couple of years older. The education she has received at the boarding school is excellent. She will do fine in evening school, probably skip grades."

When Jimmy saw how adamant his Anna was, he assumed it was because of losing her baby. He agreed.

Anna and Jimmy put a down payment on a larger brownstone on West 145th Street. They immediately built a kitchen and bathroom in the five-room downstairs area to rent. They also rented rooms upstairs. "Jimmy, *amore mio,*" Anna said, now switching easily from English to Italian to catch his attention, "a room will be used for my extra business, maybe guests."

"Yes, I know, but I want to rent to people without children. Remember what we decided."

"Fine, but remember you said also my niece could come. And the extra money I earn will help pay for her trip." Anna's voice thickened as it occurred to her he might withdraw his offer to have Marti live with them.

"Jimmy, I have to tell you the truth." She began to cross and uncross her legs under the dining room table.

"*Sì?*"

"Jimmy, Marti is my daughter," she got out the words, her eyes showing both anger and shame. Angry to be stuck having to take responsibility for Marti after the father never took responsibility for what he had done—she was barely fourteen at the time she became pregnant, he eighteen. And angry, too, because her sister, Tulia, was upset with her about their father banning from the house the young man, Tulia's suitor, after he got Anna pregnant.

"Figliodi puttana!" Anna barked a phrase Jimmy had taught her. Bitter, too, was she because her father made her feel shame and never forgave her. And, finally, she was angrier than ever because of her present shame she thought she had overcome. Yes, by working many years. All those years to support Marti while she was attending the Catholic boarding school!

Damn those hypocrites—the men who trick girls into sleeping with 'em and those nuns who are teaching my daughter to hate me because I am not the Virgin Mary! God dam them all! She looked so angry that Jimmy thought carefully before he let her know his feelings.

"Jimmy asked, lowering his voice. "Tell me what happened?"

21

He remembered with so much relief that his previous girlfriend had not become pregnant.

As Anna explained, Jimmy listened carefully, pulling at his suspenders, his face appearing stern. He felt some relief that the child was not from the man he knew Anna was writing to.

"Grazie al cielo," he said under his breath.

"Yes, she should come, but it would be better to continue the story that she is your niece. Her mother died. I have already mentioned to our friends that we are expecting her. You should have told me before, Anna."

Jimmy left the room and began reading the newspaper. Anna saw him stop, then staring at the wall for a long time.

"You care more for your stuck-up friends than me!"

"No, you got it wrong, Anna. I care for you, and I do want to stay, soon as man-and-wife. But you lied to me, and I don't want my friends to know that you lied."

What caught Anna by total surprise was that she agreed with his logic.

"And her papers in Cuba ... what's the mother's name on the birth certificate?" he asked gently.

"The officials knew. Everyone in my family knows, but the director of the boarding school does not know. Marti was only five, too young to board when I needed to send her away. So I told the Sisters that her grandmother had died and her father traveled, a story better than the truth." Anna sat down next to Jimmy. He tenderly put his arm around her.

"Jimmy, you do not have to stay with me. I will do fine without you." Anna all at once felt the anger again rising up at men, who had the freedom to walk away.

"I understand..." He kissed her searing cheek.

Lola frequently dropped by Anna's brownstone for a cup of café con leche when she needed a break from her beauty salon. Anna would open the clamp on the side of the hourglass-shaped silver pot and spoon the dark crystals onto the top tray, then add two cups of boiling water, draining the favor through the sieve into the bottom tray. She would heat milk in a pan until bubbles appeared. The coffee was poured into a cup, and she'd gently tilt the pan to avoid the thick top layer of milk from slipping into the cup. Sugar was added. She remembered the brown unrefined sugar in Cuba that was extracted from fibrous stalks. And then it was squeezed and shredded by stones or metal devices. Further processing would result in the white sugar that was sold in bodegas. Lola would grind her coffee beans and spoon the crystals into her *cafetera*. Sweetening her coffee, she fondly recalled the giant metal lattice-shaped sugar cane crushers.

Lola wore a hat that resembled a glengarry, a Scottish cap with a hanging band, similar to the one that adorned Mae West in a popular magazine photo.

"Did you see the new Mae West movie, Anna?"

"No, I haven't..." Anna sat contently reading the daily newspaper, a habit she had for most of her life. The paper's odor was familiar to those who sat by her. Her eyes pinched tightly, taking in Lola's wine-colored tight skirt, matching shoes, and oddly-shaped matching hat.

"I like her—she's comfortable being a woman and talking about how a woman feels about lovemaking. You know, instead of hiding like so many women do," said Lola. Anna smiled.

"I knew I wanted an *amante bueno* so I allowed my husband— then boyfriend—to love me even before we married. I tried him out. *Mi amante* did just fine. *Tu sabes los negros son mas dolce!*"

"You were lucky to find Carlos without tasting the bitter fruit," Anna said. As a girl, she hadn't been told about physical desire and remembered the sounds coming from her parents' bedroom --- sounds of pain and urgency, then louder cries... and silence. When she was thirteen, her sister's boyfriend would hug and kiss her when he came to their house. The young man lived in town and his father owned a bodega. He came to buy tobacco from her father's small tobacco patch and enjoyed Tulia's attention.

"The region, Abajo Vuelto, was known for its fine tobacco leaves. My great-grandfather was one of the tobacco farmers who fled the Havana area when the government cracked down because of the farmers' insistence on higher prices---and the right to sell to the public. The English, yes, took control of Havana for a year but then lost it later to the Spaniards. They paid better prices for hides, tobacco, and sugar. When the English left, my great-grandfather started to sell locally," Anna explained the best she could.

"When my sister was not around, her friend, boyfriend and I would talk. One day he came when no one was home and started hugging and kissing me. It felt good. He came again when no one was home. This time he pushed me onto Tulia's bed and kissed my neck and touched my breasts. Then he laid on top of me and pulled down my underpants. I felt this terrible pain between my legs. He would not stop. I jumped up when I was able and noticed blood on my thigh. He said not to worry, that there was no cut or anything- but not to tell anyone--- that my sister would be angry with me." Lola quickly sipped her coffee.

It was around then that Anna was sent to live with her uncle and Graciela. The boy's family never came to talk to Anna's uncaring father. This infuriated Anna's father, who felt also guilty that he had not protected his daughter. One of Anna's uncles, made

23

bitter by his job as a slave overseer, swore nothing to do with Anna. The young man was sent to Spain to study. Because newcomers were given better jobs, relationships between the Cubans and the new arrivals from Spain were already strained. Anna's pregnancy reminded her proud father of how some Spanish sailors dealt with Amerindian women during earlier times.

"Anna, tell me---why didn't you explain to your father... that you didn't like what he was doing?"

"It was impossible! You do not know my father. He even blamed my mother for not watching me closer when he was off in other provinces supervising the railroad workers." Anna quickly wiped her hands on her apron like brushing away so many pointless crumbs in her past life.

"My father blamed me- said I was loose, that I allowed it to happen. My mother blamed herself for not warning me, and I blamed her for not explaining that men do not respect women," Anna said, all the time circling one anxious thumb around the other.

"Anna, that is not true for all men. Look at your Jimmy and my husband. Carlos and I talked a lot before we shared the same bed. He wanted to be sure that I understood that he wanted to marry me, even though we did not wait until marriage. I didn't care if he decided to marry me or not. Well, I tried it before him with another boy and that one was boring!" Lola's eyes widened as she spoke. She held back a good laugh inside her puffed-up cheeks. "Women need to compare and practice before they settle on one man!" She stood up and wrapped her arms around her *querido amigo*.

3 BOARDING SCHOOL
1915 - 1925

Marti did not understand that her school would be a several hours carriage ride into the city. Majestic neoclassical buildings with columns facing open courtyards, red terra-cotta tiled roofs supported beyond the outside walls by wooden beams awed her. The balustrades overlooked opened passageways, where people scurried into during downpours. The convent was located on a narrow street, leading from a busy intersection, so much like Granada. The school's multiple floors opened toward the center courtyard. Trees and shrubs dotted the ground. The windows lacked glass but did have *barrotes*, bars constructed of wrought iron grilles, which allowed the air to circulate. Shutters closed out the night air.

"She is too young to board, but her mother is an au pair, and the grandparents live in Pinar," Sister Carmen Mary, a portly seasoned nun at fifty-five, had confided to the playful twenty-five-year-old playful Sister Beatrice. They were attired in their brown habits when the carriage driver rang the outside bell.

"The father?"

"Her mother said he travels."

"I see…" Sister Beatrice gingerly fingered around her neck the blue shield with the white cross on a chain.

"It will be difficult when her mother leaves. Let her stay in my room tonight."

Sister Carmen Mary thought: *I was right to tell good -natured Sister Beatrice. I know she would uphold the Oblate commitment of defending the rights of each family, especially of women and children!*

"I am Anna Collado de Valle," Anna said, taking the Sister's hand.

"Marti, shake the Sister's hand." The child held only Anna's hand tightly. Her eyes darted between uniform patterns on the parquetry wall panel.

"I am Sister Beatrice." She shook Anna's hand lightly. At eighteen, despite the heavy lipstick, she looked --- even wearing a uniform--- like a child herself.

"Let me show you around the school. On this level you'll find the dining room, laundry, and administrative offices. On the second level are the classrooms." She led Anna and Marti into a high-ceiling classroom, where large windows were shaded by the large palm branches outside.

"On this third floor are the dormitories, and our rooms are on the other side. Marti will share a room with eight other girls. She can take the bottom of this bunk." The Sister pointed to a metal bed.

"Here is her locker and bureau." A stand-up closet and bureau made of dented olive-colored metal. "Her roommates are at lunch. The youngest is seven and the oldest is ten. The older girls are in other rooms. Would you like to meet your roommates, Marti?"

Marti remained silent.

"Leave your bags here."

Marti continued holding her mother's hand tightly as they walked down the wide staircase lined with hanging lights fused onto chains. The faint stained glass, in flower patterns, illuminated the stairwell.

They entered a room with fifty very quiet girls between the ages of seven and eighteen. All were eating plates of rice, beans, and carne guisado, a beef stew, with root vegetables. Eight girls in school uniforms, stood up along one table.

"Good afternoon, Sister," they chanted all together.

"Sit down. This is Marti, who will share your room."

"Welcome, Marti, may God bless your stay," they chanted all aglow, almost in unison...almost. Two giggled the last words.

"You may sit down...Would you like to eat, Marti?"

Marti shook her head and stared at the girls facing straight ahead.

"Sit down, Marti," Anna whispered, looking up uneasily at the Sister.

"I want to go home, Mama, I want to see *abuela!*" she pleaded.

"No, you will stay here for a few days and on Friday we will come back for you. This will be your new home ... there will be many vacations," she added, sensing her daughter's baleful tension.

"No, Mami, I want to go with you!"

"No, I have to return to the Capitan's house," said Anna softly, an impatient edge to her voice.

"Marti, would you like to see our parakeets?" Sister Beatrice gently took Marti's hand and led her outside to a corner of the courtyard.

"Would you like to feed 'em?"

Marti nodded.

"Wait here." The Sister went to gather feed from the kitchen.

"Mama, I want to go home!" Tears streamed down Marti's face.

"I told you...we talked about this, remember ... your grandparents agreed ... you will receive a fine education here and have many girlfriends."

"But I play with my aunts."

27

"We know, but they cannot give you the education you will receive here."

"But can't I live with the children where you work?"

"No, you cannot! Besides, the whole family will be soon moving to Havana, so I will be closer and will visit often, and Julio and I will pick you up each weekend."

Marti, in tears, crumpled onto the floor. Anna stood and watched her daughter, her own tears evident when the Sister returned.

"Come, Marti," the Sister said, casually lifting her body off the floor and walking her to the center of the cages. The feathers varied from lemon yellow to turquoise blue.

"Here, do not drop these." The Sister poured a handful of seeds into Marti's palms as she opened the first cage and removed the tray. She nodded to Anna, who kissed Marti's wet cheeks and turned away.

The bond between Marti and the Sister held strong during the nine-year stay. Sister Beatrice lavished special attention on the little girl from Pinar who cried herself to sleep during her first week. Upon her return on Monday, assured that her family would always be there on weekends, she finally accepted being at the school. The comradeship of the other girls and the loving firm guidance of the Sisters helped her feel like they were like an extended family.

The Oblates had fostered schools for girls in several countries. The school's mission was to educate the poor, and particularly children of color, as the Oblates did when their schools were founded in the United States after a Cuban nun shared her vision with a progressive Frenchman. The school children were a rainbow of colors: black, white, mulatto, Chinese, and Amerindian. Their day began at 6:30 a.m. with ham and cheese on Cuban rolls and warmed milk laced with sugar and coco. Classes included math, social studies, science, language, and religion, all adapted to each specific age group.

Questioning, recitation, questioning, recitation, and such summed up the Sisters' pedagogy. There were many varied arts activities in addition to classes.

After lunch, there was chorus or household tasks, depending on the age—such as fine sewing and embroidery—where the girls chattered like the parakeets. Volunteer work promoted social justice, and biweekly dancing prepared the girls for social life.

"Marti, could you sing for the infirmed Sisters? It could be part of your service. Dear Marti, your voice is strong. Please join the chorus," Sister Beatrice asked when she heard her singing along with the phonograph while she danced. What a delight it was for Marti to dance the *danzón* with Alicia, her best friend!

Marti was thrilled to get the attention her traveling mother and grandfather could not provide. A year later, she surprised Sister Beatrice with "Sister, my father will pick me up this Friday."

On Friday a new Ford Model T with its uniformed driver, Julio, and Anna arrived.

"So nice to meet Marti's father," said Sister Beatrice, motioning Anna upstairs to gather her daughter's belongings.

"Well ... she's is like my daughter and will be officially, when Anna and I marry," said the handsome mulatto, with the longest eyelashes the Sister had ever seen. She could not help noticing him lightly twisting his moustache.

"Are you also from Pinar?"

"No, from Matanzas, but live now in Pinar. Uh, I work in the same household as Anna ... as you see ...I'm the chauffeur."

"Would you like to sit in the courtyard?"

"I...yes, thank you."

"A glass of guava?"

"Yes, thank you. The trip will be long."

"To Pinar?"

"That's so," he answered, avoiding her obvious prompting for more information.

"I will get a pitcher so everyone can have some ... you are right, the trip is long."

When Marti's returned Sunday she burst into the dining room.

"I went to my mother's workplace and played with the children. We went to the park and then ate empanadas and piraguas as a band played. My father pushed us on the swings."

"Marti, did your father visit you at your grandparents' house?"

"No, he was busy driving to the city with the Capitan."

The Sister nodded. "It is late. Come. Let's put your bag in your room and wash up before dinner. Follow me."

The routines and discipline would in-fold into Marti's personality: up at 6:30, morning prayers, then washing, breakfast, Mass, classes, lunch, afternoon activities, dinner, free play, walks through nearby streets—the girls knew not to look into the faces of passing men—and washing pads, when one's period finally came, hanging them on the outside line to dry. There were subliminal lessons too, ones that Marti did not overly notice, such as vague background radio discussions.

Stories were read and discussed regarding nationalism written by Félix Varela y Morales; the intrigues of Spanish family life by Benito Pérez Galdós; and the types of love by Cirilo Villaverde. These influences flowed through the minds of the girls like refreshing mountain streams. Tales of tragedy and heroism and passages of biblical mysterious became segments of future dreams.

Dreams! The Oblates stood by their commitment that the girls would radically transform in order to face the challenges of confronting society as women of color and to be guided by the Holy Spirit to see Christ in each person they encounter.

Marti carried these teachings with her and obeyed both the Sisters and her mother, who one day told her that she would travel to North America. And that she would send for her once she was established. Marti had grown to love her family at the boarding school. This helped... for a while.

4 MARTI COMES TO NYC
1925

Marti remembered the day she arrived in New York City. Anna met her ship from Key West at a Manhattan dock. Marti was amazed at the height of the buildings which reached to the water's edge.

"We must talk now," Anna spoke up in the trolley car on the way to a restaurant. They had oxtail stew and a cup of milk for twenty cents—the luncheon special.

"This stew has no garbanzos and is not spicy...but it smells good," Marti said. Anna quietly stared at her, amazed at how mature she looked at thirteen.

"*Sí,* they do not stick in a lot of garlic, onions, cilantro, or green pepper the way we do."

Anna asked about her boat trips, first from Havana to Key West, then from Key West to Manhattan.

"Manolo's wife was very nice, and she told me about life here. I could not eat much on the boats... my stomach was upset with the rocking."

"I changed your birthdate on the birth register so it would appear that you are two years older," Anna said, heartsick by the burden of her new responsibility. Marti's smile soon faded as well, once Anna laid down the ground rules of the household. She could

31

attend night school but like everyone else had to work during the day.

Quota laws passed in the 1920s slowed down the immigration flow. Accordingly, Marti was lucky to come to New York when she did. She noticed how much Marti spoke about missing the Sisters and classmates at the Havana school, her mind as restless as those of most teenagers.

At first, Marti did not like Jimmy. She blamed him for how long it took for Anna to send for her and for her having to work. But soon, when the Depression gripped the country, Marti would understand the value of labor and see how fair-minded he was. Jimmy and Anna gave her a comfortable room with high ceilings and a heavy mahogany door that provided quiet from the busy street. Her window overlooked the backyards of three brownstones. Marti observed that many immigrants like herself shared the neighborhood.

A week later, a friend of Jimmy's visited and met Marti. As he entered the foyer where curving steps led to the upper floor, she overheard him say to Jimmy, "It was a pleasure to meet Anna's niece."

"Anna, why didn't you tell Jimmy who I am?" Marti asked, walking into Anna's bedroom, where she was folding clothes.

"I thought we discussed this when you arrived."

"No, you just told me that I had to work, and you had fixed my papers so that I would appear to be two years older."

"That was to make it possible for you to work here. You are too young."

"I'm not talking about work. You are my mother! Why didn't you tell Jimmy that? He told his friend that I am your niece!"

Anna's body trembled. "I had to say you were my niece since that is on your immigration papers."

"But I'm your daughter!"

"Yes, you are."

"And my father visited all the time when I was at school."

"No, Julio was my boyfriend. He did not want to come to America."

"So who is my real father..?!?"

"A young boy who was my sister's boy friend. He was sent away after it happened and---"

"You lied to the Sisters---to *me*, I can't believe this!"

"Grandfather was right when he refused to have you in the house. Now I understand why! Does Jimmy know all this? Tell me!"

"Yes, but he felt we should continue calling you my niece."

"You liar!"

Jimmy heard the yelling and hurried into the bedroom.

"It was my decision to say you are Anna's niece," Jimmy said at Anna's bedside. His voice was faint. "It was my fault, not your mother's. I thought it would be better for all of us. You know, some people would not understand the situation. I wanted to protect both of you." Jimmy remained calm. He felt guilty because he had instructed Anna to continue the deception, finding it difficult to accept the truth. He was uneasy because he and Anna weren't yet married.

"She lied! I thought my father was Julio and that they had separated. Now she has a different story." Marti grabbed the doorknob for support as a wave of dizziness hit her.

Anna was disappointed that Marti lacked the maturity to put things together. "You are too young to grasp this. I did what was best for you. I am the one who worked since the age of fifteen to support you in the boarding school."

"I hate you!" Marti's face was so contorted Anna stepped back. "How can you deny that I am your daughter?" Marti's stomach was a tangle of roots. "I felt so proud of Julio when you would both pick me up from school. He looked so special in his uniform."

"How ungrateful you are! Look what we have given you!" Anna shouted, lunging at Marti. Jimmy jumped in between them. "Who is my father ?!?"

Despite Anna's tears, she seemed still. "How ungrateful you are," she mumbled to herself.

"She's still too young to understand," said Jimmy, who believed the thirteen-year-old. Marti was still a child. "She doesn't realize that she has a better future here." "Yes, and she arrived just before immigration was tightened."

"You are a bad woman!"

"I did not know any better at the time."

"Why did my grandparents lie?"

"My father hated me for what had happened. He insisted we never talk about it," cried out Anna.

"You will pay for your sins!"

"Marti, didn't they teach you to respect your mother at that school?" *All this humiliation.* She disliked Marti for it and felt betrayed by her father and by Julio, who refused to join her in New York.

The argument grew into a cacophony of opera-like lyrics full of shame and doubt.

Over the years the lie would persist through many generations:

"She is my aunt," Marti would lie to her school friends.

"My sister died birthing her daughter. We are like mother and daughter," Anna shaded the story.

"You mean she was my grandmother, not a great aunt?!" Marti's grown son, Alfredo Jr., decades later would shout in a crowded restaurant. The family thought he had known.

"Women's oppression... women blame themselves, not the system," her granddaughter, Norma, would say sixty years later.

The grand opera played over and over. Marti did grow to love Jimmy—how he cringed his lips, narrowed his eyes, and pulled at his hauberk suspenders—but she resigned herself to be ashamed of her mother's actions--- and of being born out of wedlock.

Marti channeled her anger into her work. She changed jobs frequently whenever a higher salary was offered. She remembered when she was applying for a position the manager of one garment factory who haughtily told her that there was no work. Then he changed his mind when he heard her whispering in Spanish about how rude *he* was. He did call her back. His prejudice lashed out like a rattler's tongue against those of color who spoke English over Spanish-speaking immigrants. In this factory, Marti worked alongside other immigrant women who had learned sewing skills in their homelands.

Marti learned Italian because only Spanish and Italian were spoken at home. Her ears picked up musical rhythms as well as foreign words. She attended night classes to study English and completed middle school, graduating at sixteen.

When she studied the lyrics of Italian operas at home, Jimmy enjoyed correcting her pronunciation. Marti's strong mezzo-soprano voice would shake the walls when she practiced popular songs while washing the dishes.

She steadily grew to understand New York culture and dreamed of singing at downtown concert halls. But eager to please her "aunt's" rule that "we all work here," she stoically crocheted flag and eagle emblems on military hats whose wingspan curved around the hat's brim.

In addition to crocheting, knitting, and cooking, her Cuban boarding school had awakened her mind to philosophy, science, math, and history.

Knowing these subjects it was easier to pass night classes. Marti remembered so well how the stern Oblate Sisters could inflict psychological cruelty if their rules were not followed. "Walk in a straight line when on the street... A woman is to be obedient to her husband." Marti had unpleasant thoughts about people who fell below the Oblate Sisters' standards, perhaps motivated by her own shame and anger about *being nacido fuera del matrimonio*. The feeling was driven in like nails by an Irish coworker who spoke of the harsh workhouses for unwed pregnant women run by the nuns in her native country.

Marti's thoughts often flowed back to her nine-year stay at the convent. In town, women dressed in long skirts, some holding opened umbrellas, deeply engaged in the talk of the day with friends--- or more often with family members. Men sported pointed boots, fitted dark pants, and guayabera shirts. They enjoyed stopping at a stand to purchase thick café negro. They chatted about newspaper stories, sports, or the women who passed by. Horse-driven carts or buggies, and the rare automobile, filled the air with dust. It was much different in New York, Marti realized. Women here were very direct, like Selma.

Marti's new friend Selma, a spunky twenty-five-year-old daughter of immigrants from Poland, was as outspoken as Anna's friend Lola. She wore the latest fashions; crochet hats on her bobbed-cut hair, and below-the-knee dresses. She spoke with a "lisp" owing to protruding upper teeth that called attention to her mouth. Which emitted a steady stream of commentary, as though it were an engine warming up. Her father was a tailor and her mother worked as a cashier in their neighborhood butcher shop.

"Marti, listen, there's a union meeting. Tonight. We have concerns about the heavy doors that lock if they're shut by accident. Remember those girls who died in that Shirtwaist factory fire in the City here!"

"No, I don't know about that. What is shirtwaist?" asked Marti, busy knotting yellow silk thread before beginning the black outline of the insignia.

"Those popular blouses usually buttoned in back, puffy sleeves, and narrow at the waist. Poor working conditions led to over 140 women dying."

"Dios mio!"

"Yes, according to the workers, doors were bolted from the outside, to protect the loss of fabric. It was a safety violation. Many people think that the doors were also locked to block the entrance of union organizers. The fire ladders didn't reach the upper floors. Horrible! The women were trapped surrounded by cotton scraps, tissue paper patterns, and wooden tables."

"Oh, my God!" Do the fire ladders reach these floors now?"

"Yes... things have improved. Now we have a union to voice our concerns. That's why these meetings are damn important."

"I have to ask my aunt first if I can go."

"Where do you live?"

"West 156th Street."

"Me, on 168th Street. I can stop at your house before going downtown."

"Your parents won't know where you are."

"Marti, they know I'm going out to dinner and then to the meeting. Please join us for dinner Selma, okay?"

Selma recognized where Marti lived, the front of the

brownstone's wrought iron fence circling the downstairs entrance brownstone. The shop of her butcher was located nearby. Selma ate rice, black beans, and *ropa vieja*, scraping her plate. Anna asked her if she wanted seconds.

"Not now... thank you, Anna."

"Jimmy, I assume you belong to a union?"

"Yes, the fabric dyers. I will soon be a silk dyer specialist."

Marti listened intently, surprised how interested everyone was in unions. Jimmy explained that one of the reasons he had moved out of his Italian village, so feudalistic with no unions.

Marti envied Selma's outspokenness during the meeting that was located at the union hall. There, she went over the need to have women on the executive board. Marti's "ladylike" restraint was rooted in her boarding school upbringing, but on this night she felt part of the American culture.

"Marti, great, there's a movie playing with Pedro de Cordoba at the Roxy. You know he is Cuban," Shelma said the following day on their lunch break.

"True, Shelma, but only on his father's side. His mother is French. He is very handsome and perfect for silent pictures."

They went to the movies frequently, joining the fifty percent of other Americans. So many, all different: *They Saw It* with Clara Bow, *The King of Kings* directed by Cecil B. DeMille; *The Jazz Singer*, with Al Jolson, the first moving pictures show; and the Marx Brothers in *Coconuts*.

Yes, there's a rainbow lurking
Lurking behind the clouds
Shouting to move the rains
A rainbow to warm our hearts
A rainbow of joy to watch
After the dark clouds part
Filling this dame with joy
As my love, parting the clouds.
As my love, an umbrella for rains."

Marti sang with gusto while finishing the dishes. Thinking about a movie, she didn't know that she would soon be falling in love.

5 BOARDERS
1929 - 1930

Anna and Jimmy with Friends

Anna and Jimmy had the downstairs of their brownstone converted into a rental unit by Tony. He was a twenty-eight -year-old jovial and short Cuban American carpenter from Long Island. Tony enjoyed dances thrown by Marti and her girlfriends. He had divorced a woman from Andalusia whose family thought she should marry a professional-- not a carpenter whose family was from Cuba, not Spain. Because he had a son, Tony Jr., Tony continued to work mostly on Long Island, but he preferred life in

Manhattan, visiting it often. Tony had mentioned to Anna and Jimmy that a family member of his might be interested in renting.

A medium-built, oval-faced, handsome man in his mid-thirties appeared at the door soon after the rental was available to ask about the two-bedroom apartment in Anna and Jimmy's brownstone. *"Mi cuñado* (brother-in-law*), Tony, dijo que hay un apartamento aquí."* He had only to say a few words before Anna recognized his Gallego-tinged Cuban accent.

"Tony told us you live in Tampa," said Anna, before inviting him into the hall. His narrow brown eyes fixed on her, while his genuine-looking smile charmed her from the first.

"Yes. My wife is still in Tampa, and I came because our daughter needs an operation on a damaged leg. Tony offered a bed in his house, but we prefer to live near the Columbia Presbyterian Hospital area."

"Did she have an accident?"

"No, she was born with a hip problem that caused her leg to turn in."

"Anna, they will be staying only until after the surgery. Tony's brother-in-law has been promised a super's job in a few months," Jimmy confided after the man left. "They are Cubans."

"But you said no children," an amused Anna said.

"It will be for a short time. Evangelista and Juan are Cubans," he repeated.

Anna went back to her *Look* magazine. She frowned, thinking there was no way to change this man's mind.

After lovely Evangelista, Juan, and their daughter moved into the brownstone, the family began to fill an empty hole in Anna and Jimmy's hearts. Anna and Jimmy would much later become the godparents of one of their girls. Juan began to play cards with Jimmy. One evening it was poker in the living room. Its tables were beautifully adorned by Anna's contour map-like embroidery.

"You win again!" exploded Juan while straightening his precisely knotted tie.

Jimmy pulled at his suspenders in agreement, then sipped a shot of rum, loosening his tongue like a lever. "I'm thinkin' of buying a new car, Juan."

"A car! Can we afford one?!?" called out Anna from the sofa.

"Yes." Jimmy shot her a missile-like glance. "I want to buy a Buick. It has rear coil suspension for a smoother ride." Anna returned to reading the newspaper, tilting her head to eavesdrop.

"This year, they have installed rear-turn signals."

"Have you considered a Chevrolet? It has a silent valve in the head engines, synchronized transmissions, about $659. If you can afford to buy a new car, the Chevrolet is as good as any one of them. At least you know it's guaranteed for part failures."

Jimmy liked Juan's sensibility. Several days later, he met him walking up the front stairs and invited him for coffee. "Hey, Juan, how are you!"

Jimmy was happy to have a visitor. Juan was five years older than him and read books from the library as well as the daily newspaper. Jimmy boiled water and made two cups of espresso.

"Sit down. My wife's at the hairdresser." He led Juan into their kitchen, proud of its high ceiling, built-in oak cupboards, and Glenwood enamel gas stove. And that white porcelain icebox lined with galvanized steel!

"You know the movie *The Jazz Singer*? The newspaper said it's the end of the silent films. We have seen many changes in recent years." Jimmy continued heating the milk until it began to boil, and then poured it over the coffee.

"Yes, we see many changes. Did you read about the Cristero War in Mexico? The pro-church rebels attacked the government?"

"Why did they do that, Juan?"

"The government banned the Catholic faith."

"That religion was dumped on the Mexican Indians. Damn, are we sendin' troops to help the Mexican government?"

"No. President Coolidge seems 'preoccupied.' You know, he's not running again."

"I hadn't read about that," Jimmy said sipping his coffee slowly. How he enjoyed the company of this thoughtful, educated man. He set his cup on the tablecloth. "Hey, Juan, did you read about those two Italians who were executed 'cause of their union activity?"

"Yeah, some people don't like unions."

"Sure, usually the bosses," Jimmy chuckled.

"Look, the bosses make the money, and we workers are expected to remain quiet and take what they hand out. I took the lead at the company and invested in stocks last year. Well, guess what? They're not doing too good."

"Man, I don't get it, Juan. Why don't you just keep cash in the bank?"

"Because I make more, Jimmy, with stocks than from the interest in the savings bank. All the congressmen own stocks, y' know."

"Okay..." Jimmy stood up. "But they know what to buy with information we regular workers never get."

"Yes, remember that scandal in the early twenties? What was it called ... the pot ... no, the teapot scandal."

"... Dome scandal, Juan ... maybe tea dome or Teapot Dome scandal. A guy in the president's own cabinet was involved."

"Well, what happened?"

"Loans were made on the sly--under the table--to the Secretary of the Interior. He hired companies without similar bids."

"O.K. Then how much money was involved?"

Jimmy sat down, straightening his tie again. "Hundreds of thousands of dollars, Juan.... You hungry?" Jimmy felt his own stomach growling.

"Sure, what did your amazing Anna concoct today?"

"Oxtail stew and a flan."

"Hey, you don't have to ask me again!" Jimmy opened the icebox, got the stew, and heated it on the stove. He was lucky to have a friend with whom he could discuss barring any reservations on any subject. Their favorite topics? Their work, sports, and politics.

In 1929 when Wall Street crashed, the floor smashed out from under them.

"Hoover isn't allowing the government to step in as he should!"

" Well, the money's not gonna come down to the regular working person."

Juan knew this firsthand. He lost every cent in the stock market. Jimmy had blown his savings. But he and Anna had just bought a brownstone building near 134th Street and Broadway, and most of his money was invested there. Wiped out was the question of Marti leaving work to attend high school full time. So were the savings of many people.

Anna sat in her rocking chair, reading the newspaper. "Thirteen million, no jobs. We are lucky that we're working and that we can collect from our boarders."

6 MARTI MEETS ALFREDO
1931 - 1932

Marti first saw him in 1931 in Anna's kitchen, soaking his swollen feet in a black-and-white metal roasting pan. Alfredo, fed up with milking cows in Tampa, had moved to New York. His first job was pulling garment racks between factories in Manhattan, where trucks lined streets, smoke curled up from dangling cigarettes as men unloaded wire racks of clothing that hung like beef. You could see and feel them maneuvering between pedestrians, and tin buildings filled with clothing, notions, and bolts of leaning fabric. Tony would work in carpentry, while his brother Cuco was a postman, Nick was a career army officer, and their parents' fourth son, Ramon, would later purchase several delivery trucks to rent. Only one of Tony's brothers attended college while in the service. Evangelista, the oldest sister, was the first to arrive in New York.

Marti, two years older than Alfredo, felt more drawn to this young man than to any other since coming to New York. She circled around him like a buzzing bird of prey.

"Anna suggested I soak my feet. Both ankles are swollen, too many hours of walking. Epsom salt reduces swelling," he explained, feeling uncomfortable that his feet were sitting in a metal pan.

"Who are you? The new boarder?" She was barely able to control her laughter.

"Nope, I was visiting my sister, Evangelista, in her apartment downstairs. Anna stopped by and insisted I come to her place, and she would show me how to soak my swollen ankles."

"Just adding some flavor to Anna's soup," he sang out as Marti walked away toward her room, thinking: *So, this is the younger brother from Tampa.*

Alfredo shared his sister's wit and love of gabbing. He was five-foot-seven, thin, and built like a wiry tennis player. Actually, he had played baseball in a Tampa minor league, despite the damage to his heart from his childhood rheumatic fever. A thin mustache shadowed his curved lips. He also had a Roman nose, friendly brown eyes, a high forehead, and thick wavy black hair – which he kept brushed back. His Amerindian slanted eyes narrowed and sparkled when he spoke. He liked Marti instantly, unaware that she was being courted for a year by Jimmy's second cousin, Joseph.

Jimmy wrote letters to his family after arriving to New York. His father, who had been elected their hometown's (San Sostene) mayor, shortly thereafter became gravely ill with diphtheria. Jimmy booked a passage for them on an Italian ship, but his father died en route. Too expensive a trip for Anna, she was left behind to take care of their boarders.

In Italy Jimmy met his second cousin, who planned to emigrate to New York. Jimmy's mother, who lived near two married sisters, understood that her son loved his new country. Later, Joseph frequently visited his sponsor, Jimmy, in New York. Marti welcomed the attention of Joseph, who was much older than she at thirty-four. But did not have fun with him, as she did with Alfredo. Before Joseph, Marti had no boyfriends who measured up to her high standards, her busy work schedule, and night school. Still, Marti, enjoying the company of her girlfriends, was not lonely for company. She had begun studying music at night school and helped by Jimmy, her command of Italian made it easier to sing the scores of operas like *La Bohème*. While Joseph was as practical and organized as was Marti, he was uninterested in Italian opera. He would visit every Friday night at six for dinner. Afterward, he would play cards with Jimmy or go to the movies with Marti and one of her parents. Occasionally, when she was chaperoned by one of her girlfriends, Joseph would hold Marti's hand.

"Want to go to the movie, Marti?" Alfredo blurted out. Not allowed out alone, she invited her girlfriend, Beatrice, to come along. Alfredo, joined by his brother Tony, met her in front of her building. "I have a special day planned for us," Alfredo said, tucking his arms into theirs.

"Oh, which movie?"

"It's a surprise, Beatrice. Don't ask! We'll make one stop before."

Marti introduced Beatrice to Tony.

She tiptoed lightly: "Are you a friend?"

"Not a friend... I'm Alfredo's bodyguard."

"Ha, Ha. Come on, who are you, really?"

"I'm really his brother. Though some days I think his real mother, scared by his birth, threw him on our doorstep."

Alfredo pushed his older brother, and they pretended to fist fight.

"Marti, he looks like that famous artist," Beatrice whispered.

"Yeah, Pablo Picasso. He's like an artist. He learned carpentry and can design and make even furniture like an artist."

Their first stop was Thirty-fourth Street, where they stood in a long line. "Ladies, you are going to enter the tallest building in the world, 1,250 feet, 102 stories ... the Empire State Building!" called out Alfredo with pride.

Marti could not believe the view. She kept telling Alfredo to be quiet when he repeatedly "threatened to jump" if they didn't go to lunch after the movie.

A man with a heavy Brooklyn accent, pressing against them in the mob, prompted, "Ah, jeez, go to lunch with him." The movie he chose was *Dracula*. Marti squeezed Alfredo's hand in fear, and he kept holding onto hers. She felt his staring, but was too shy to steal a glance at him. She giggled. When Beatrice left for the bathroom, Alfredo leaned over and kissed her cheek. He smiled a little when their eyes met. Afterward, a blushing Marti took side peeks at him throughout the evening. A stirring of warmth resided in her hidden place.

"We are going to lunch? Oooo... Spiders, anyone?" Alfredo's voice and gestures mimicked Dracula all the way to Horn & Hardart Automat, New York's early version of vending machines. Picking up a handful of nickels, Alfredo asked the cashier where the rice and beans were. Each compartment of food, surrounded by a sliding glass door, held one item, which was surrendered by inserting the correct number of nickels into a slot and then twisting a knob. Open sesame!

"We don't have that, but we do have fresh macaroni and cheese," she replied with a wry smile, her rubber- tipped finger pointing to the glass surrounded tray.

"Thank you, precious," Alfredo said to the cashier, who adjusted her chair to watch the group's selections.

Alfredo inserted the money and the tray turned in front of the door. He slid it open.

"Let me try!" Marti enjoyed purchasing meatloaf and potatoes. "I'll have the fish sticks, then coleslaw ... Oh, look at that apple pie too." happy Beatrice piped up.

Alfredo's turn in a soothing tone, "Sit down, ladies, I'll buy the drinks."

"He is so cute, just like a teddy bear," whispered Beatrice again. Marti smiled and breathed in all the good fun she was having with Alfredo. Although he was younger, he was so easy with everyone, like with the American cashier.

Alfredo came to visit Marti's apartment so often that Anna started to cook extra on Saturdays. He came once on Friday, when Joseph was there, but left quickly. Juan and Jimmy remained mum about what was going on between Marti and Alfredo. Anna and Evangelista did not. Anna had found out about Alfredo's damage and remembered how swollen his ankles were.

"He is ill, and Marti should not invest her future. How long can he work? We all must work during this Depression," she concluded after reading in the newspaper that its tight grip would be around for a long while. Despite Anna's strong measure of doubt, nature prevailed like a leaf's crimson colors in autumn and Alfredo's frequent visits continued.

Evangelista imagined "a nice" Polish-American girl who worked in Alfredo's factory would be better for him, as two of her brothers had married Americans. Would it make him more American?

"That Polish girl, Paula, is a bookkeeper, a good job," she said matter of factly. Alfredo ignored her. His sister was too much in his business. "She does not know how to prepare pasteles. You married a Cuban yourself," he later confided to Evangelista.

"But Juan's family in Florida and Cuba are fairly well off. One of his past relatives was the captain of the *Niña*, which accompanied Columbus in the late 1400s to Cuba."

"Well, *my* relative met him when he landed in Cuba and gave him directions where to go." That was directed to Juan; Alfredo deciding it would be better to shut his mouth as far as his oldest sister was concerned.

Evangelista, of course, knew too well about the struggles her Spanish-born husband had after the Cuban War of Independence when Spain lost control of Cuba. Juan wanted to learn to fly planes in the Cuban military, but now Spaniards were excluded. She said, "Now we face difficulties because we are Spanish among these Americans." She was an ambitious woman.

"Alfredo, you spend so much time upstairs," Evangelista mentioned weeks later.

"Marti? You mean her?"

His reply sailed right past her.

"Paula asked for you when I met her at the fish market."

Alfredo drew in his breath at her casual hints.

"I'm not marrying an American."

" Come on, did I say to?"

"Why, then, tell me, do you always bring up Paula? "Paula--Paula--Paula! I will marry who pleases *me*, not *you*."

"But Alfredo, we are now in America . . . We are Spanish . . ."

Alfredo raised his voice. "No, we are Cubans!"

"But our grandfather is a Spaniard."

"Yes, because he was born in Andalusia."

Alfredo really wanted to drop the discussion, so he knew his comeback would annoy his sister:

"But our mother is Cuban: She has that salt and pepper mix in her family. Our father came from Spain, where Moors lived for many centuries."

"The Moors came from Arabia."

"No, Evangelista. Moors came from Northern Africa. They brought backward Spain a water collection system and invited doctors and teachers. Why do I always have to repeat myself, sister? You treat me like I don't know anything just because you're older!" His voice got even louder. He was annoyed that she had absorbed the attitudes of racist Americans and elitist Spaniards.

"Well ... why did the Spanish throw out the Moors?"

To him, Evangelista was obviously waffling. "They were a different religion not Catholic!"

"Anyway, Paula is a very nice girl." Evangelista couldn't refute her brother.

Entering the room, it was easy for Juan to overhear the conversation. "Marti is a very good girl, too," he said in a calm, diplomatic tone.

They all remained silent.

Juan was a practical man who thought before he spoke, unlike Evangelista who allowed her emotions to color her words.

"Look, let him marry whoever he loves. I loved you and have been very happy," said Juan later, looking up from reading the newspaper.

Juan thought his wife was as silly as some of the Americans he'd meet in the building that he supervised. But, nevertheless, he acted toward them according to his principles: *Treat all people with dignity and they will do the same to you... usually,* he thought, his face lit-up.

Marti liked joking with Alfredo, who shared her cultural history. She was keenly aware of the prejudices of the times and wished to remain in the comfort zone of another Cuban-American who having grown up in Tampa, knew how to negotiate his way around in this culture. Alfredo loved gospel church music, which resembled Santería music to the Cubans. He inhaled American cigarettes, was familiar with slang, and came from a family of many children. So he knew how to get along with different personalities.

Marti's English was halting, as her family spoke only Spanish or Italian at home, and she was afraid of the rough language and behavior of the people she met in New York. She felt they did not share the refined manners that were hammered into her by the nuns at the boarding school. Anna was thankful for Marti's fear of wandering outside the family, as it made it easier to sway Marti. Still, Anna privately made fun of Marti's excessive manners, a defense shield she had maneuvered to control her own deep - seated feelings of clawing anger.

Anna's memories never left her about the Capitan's lessons on feelings. He would dismiss her attempts at not sharing her true feelings. So he encouraged Anna to verbally express her anger at the children when they were naughty. He taught her that manners did not help working women, who needed to learn to stand up for themselves. Anna developed "an attitude" with people she perceived crossed her. One time a woman in Manhattan pushed her baby carriage defiantly in front of Anna's car after the light had turned green. She had caught Anna's critical eye, stuck her nose in the air, and walked into the intersection --- baby carriage in front. Anna slammed on the brakes, jumped out of the car, ran after the astonished woman, and shouted, "Go to Hell, *estúpida!* You no care for car hit baby!" She slapped the woman in the face and hurriedly drove away.

Alfredo enjoyed hearing Anna's bountiful stories about her adventures, but Jimmy remained aloof, wishing that Marti eventually would marry Joseph. On Saturdays, Alfredo would invite Marti and any available sibling to go to the Roxy Movie Theatre, where they absorbed two or three movies. *Flash Gordon* was by far their favorite. After one movie, Alfredo remained unusually quiet during their walk and trolley ride to Marti's house.

They were sitting on the stoop of her brownstone when Alfredo's words tumbled out: "Marti, I lost five hundred dollars when the banks went bankrupt. But could we get engaged anyway?"

"Are you serious?"

"No, Marti, just practicing my speech, y' know. For when I find someone that I may wish to marry," he said softly, touching her cheek.

Marti stifled a bigger smile. "Let me think about it. This is so sudden."

Later, in her room, her scrambled thoughts gave her no relief: *Do I want to marry now? Since I arrived from Cuba people have told me what to do: You must work; must go to school, but only if there is time. Working is what's most important since the Depression, you know. You cannot study singing. That is for rich girls. It is not safe to go downtown by yourself. You cannot go to parties without Anna or someone from the family. What do I want?*

Marti couldn't sleep, so she sat by the window watching the shadows eclipsed by brownstones extend onto the backyard. She always had wanted a large family and Alfredo had one. They would add their own children to the family. She dreamed of singing but knew the difficulties that came with singing professionally. *I have enough common sense not to take that risk!* She veered her thinking to other things and then tried to distract herself by turning off her brain--- picking up a magazine and flipping one page after another:

Hems have dropped to the ankles, long skirts, just like what these movie stars are wearing. Everyone's reading about glamorous people, she thought, trying to stay clear of her pressing personal issue. The life of a singer was not so glamorous, a lot of late nights and traveling. She tossed the magazine down, feeling that as a married lady she was better off singing at the club, at weddings, or maybe at church. They have a choir that sings at our church, she vividly recalled.

What if I got pregnant? Marti wondered with a soft giggle or two, as she beheld the rising moon. She thought about how Anna had suffered from having a baby before she got married and how hard it was on her because of it. A cat jumped on the window ledge across the yard, peering straight at her.

Marti decided not to take any chances by waiting. "I see how Evangelista brings over those single American girls for Alfredo. One brother has married a Polish girl. Alfredo is so much fun to be with, even though Anna thinks he's sick. If he takes his medicine, he will be all right. Yes, I will take good care of him, my Alfredo: my *Cubanito*," she spoke out loud to the cat watching it all with feline intensity.

Railing against the marriage, Anna yelled, "Marti, you're marrying a hospital bed!"

"*Mira*, my wife, let them engage and marry too, if they love each other. I loved you and have been very happy with *my* decision."

7 MARRIAGE
1933 - 1934

They were married in 1933 in the Church of Esperanza on West 165th Street in Manhattan. Evangelista helped Marti sew her wedding dress, each stitch in perfect place. Alfredo and his bride were exhausted from the day's activities, including preparing for the wedding; the ceremony followed by Mass; the nearby photo session; and back to the church reception hall. There, the family and friends ate and drank. A lively seven-piece Cuban band hired by Anna and Jimmy revved up favorite dance tunes.

Tony had invited Beatrice to the wedding. "My brother is gaining a beautiful wife, and she is gaining a large family. Be aware, we will ask for a room for the night sometimes," chortled Nick, as his petite Puerto Rican wife smiled demurely at her handsome husband.

"Alfredo, I just want to say that you are the best baseball player--- and fisherman--- in the family. You hooked a beautiful fish, and here's a toast to happiness, and health." Waves of assenting nods spread through the reception hall." And many little fishes!" exclaimed his brother Ramon, who would eventually father five "fishes" with his South American wife. According to the family gossip, she once flung open the window of their apartment during an argument and shouted repeatedly to passersby and neighbors, "Ramon Galindez is a bastard!"

Marti and Alfredo kissed each time they heard the glasses clink, had a wonderful time, and left the party early for a three-hour ride to Atlantic City. A short honeymoon. It was the busy season, so Alfredo had to be back to work on Tuesday.

For their honeymoon Alfredo had chosen a boarding house that his fellow worker recommended. It was built at the turn of the century, near the boardwalk. Other union members from New York frequented it. Alfredo knew that some Americans preferred their own hotels. The area was dotted with sturdy wooden boarding houses. Their patio overlooked the ocean. He planned on visiting Grace's Little Belmont, which was nearby, to hear organ music woven into jazz, but they ended up camped out in their hotel room most of the time.

Alfredo got the key and carried the suitcases into their room. He dropped the suitcases and suddenly swept Marti onto the bed. He lay next to her, huffing vigorously. Alarmed, she asked if it was his heart.

"No, it's from picking up a cow-sized woman...."

Relieved, she threw some pillows at him, and soon a full-blown pillow fight filled the air. They kissed a long time. She suddenly jumped up from Alfredo's embrace.

"Close the door, *hombre!*"

"Yes, I am your *hombre,*" he replied, standing up and bouncing on the bed.

"Alright, hombre."

He stood up and jumped up and down on the bed.

"Alright, hombre," she repeated softer, looking out the window to where the ocean had turned multiple colors from the sunset. "Let's take a walk on the beach *amor mio,*" she suddenly said. They did for about thirty minutes, feeling the gravely sand under their feet as dusk approached, talking about the wonderful day. Marti sang on, to the last of the sun.

When they returned to their room, Alfredo suggested it was time to order in food. He scoured the *Yellow Pages* as Marti crouched in a nearby chair, her eyes following him intently. Then she stood up and unpacked.

He followed her cue. "Uh, how 'bout the food?"

"How 'bout I go into the bathroom and change into something Lola gave me?"

"Sure, I'll change here into something I got at Sal's Army and Navy Store."

Marti returned from the bathroom in a salmon-colored negligee. She quickly dropped under the covers. Alfredo, now in his World War I green T-shirt and khaki shorts, trotted over to her.

She bent down a bit. "I have been very curious about how this works, Alfredo." Marti hugged him, then kissed his cheek.

"Well, don't worry about that. It comes naturally. You know God wanted us all to bring baby ducks and other creatures into this world, or we would not have duck soup." He licked her nose, cheeks, neck, and then lifted her nightgown. "Oh, there they are."

He removed his shirt and shorts and slid off her nightgown, kissing her belly.

She stiffened as he caressed her thigh. "You can kiss mine first," he said, which she did ... quickly.

"Your thing is very hairy, *mi amor.*"

"Yes, to keep me warm. Let me look at yours. Oh, it's hairy also, reminds me of a bush out in the desert with its curves of sand dunes. And you don't have the thing I have. What d'you think? Was it cut off by the nuns at your school?"

"Alfredo, the nuns did conduct classes about the differences and what men and women do."

"The question I would ask is have you tried it?"

"Oh, Alfredo, you are *so* fresh."

"What did the priest say when the nun came to him during confession? 'Oh Father, I have sinned. I allowed Father Pedro to kiss me.' Maybe... well, Sister, you must repeat five Hail Mary's, but don't let him get into the habit!'"

A shuddering laugh, then she closed her eyes as Alfredo licked first her left thigh, then the area above her bush, then the middle of her bush. He looked up, "I still can't find my keys."

They cuddled as he caressed her tightly and allowed God's wish for humankind to continue.

Their lovemaking exploration went on for another hour. They ordered Chinese food, relishing it in bed, she in his shirt, and he in his World War I shorts. They continued their zestful pleasure for the rest of the night, until they fell blissfully asleep.

When they returned to New York, they moved into the two-bedroom apartment that Evangelista and Juan vacated after they took a building superintendent job. The job was perfect for Alfredo's fastidious sister, known to iron her own sheets and during lunchtime change the clothes of her two daughters. Now she swept the foyer twice daily. Not so unusual for the oldest of many siblings. She helped her mother, Gertrudis, with the housework. After Evangelista married, her mother became pregnant again.

Marti felt proud of her handsome husband and her new extended family. But within one month, while he was walking to the bathroom in his shorts, she noticed his swollen ankles. They dressed and took a cab to the emergency room. Following tests, Alfredo was admitted. He remained in the hospital for two weeks for treatments to stop his heart's arrhythmia. Marti lit candles each day in the Church of Esperanza, where in a darkened corner stood a tray with forty metal candleholders. Inside the colored miniature glasses, light cast a glow onto kneeling Marti, who chose a few candles and lit them with a long thick reed while asking God to protect Alfredo. She dropped coins that landed with a pop against the metal tray bottom.

"Anna was right. You are a sick man," Marti let slip out during one hospital visit. Then she broke down in her husband's arms.

"Look, Marti, I didn't know the heart problem would continue. Some people with rheumatic heart disease live without problems. I kept on thinking I would get better." He faced Marti fully, hoping to wipe away the disappointment from her eyes. Alfredo spent two months at home that winter. Part of the time he rested in Key West with family and friends.

Marti confided in Selma when they were walking home from work. "I hadn't expected Alfredo to be away so long. I did not realize he was so ill. Maybe I married too fast, Selma. He could become an invalid."

"I had a cousin in Poland who married a woman with a heart condition."

"Did she become an invalid?"

"No, she died."

"Oh, Selma, you really know how to cheer somebody up!"

"Marti, when you marry you take what you get. Frank is no prize, but it could be worse. You make the best of what you got."

Easy for her to say, Marti thought. *Her husband is robust and healthy.* Marti invited Selma and Frank over for pot roast that night.

Frank cracked jokes over dinner. "A wise Jewish man of Chelm came to the rabbi with a question. 'Why is it,' he asked, 'that a slice of bread with butter on it always falls with the buttered side down?' 'Is that so?' asked the rabbi. ' So let's see if it's true.' The rabbi buttered a piece of bread and let it fall. This time the buttered side was facing up. 'Now, what about that?' asked the rabbi. 'But, Rabbi,' came the reply, 'you obviously buttered the wrong side!'"

After the ripples of laughter subsided Marti spoke as she brought out a bread pudding. "I heard one from my girlfriend who runs a beauty salon. See, this lady goes to her beautician to have her hair done and tells her she is going on a cruise to Italy on the Royal Ship Tours, staying in Hotel Rome, looking forward to dining at the famous spiffy Naples restaurant, and touring the Vatican."

Frank flicked his hand for her to go on.

"The beautician says back, 'That cruise line has poor accommodations on board, that hotel is known for its filthy rooms, that restaurant may be out of business once in a while due to poor management. And those Vatican tours are really boring, one religious painting after another. Anyway, that is what my clients tell me.' "

Selma was now urging Anna to continue.

"After two months, the customer returns to have her hair done again. 'Well, sweetheart, how was your trip?' the beautician asks. "There were fewer people than the ship's captain expected, and we were upgraded to First Class. What a suite we stayed in! Then the hotel had been renovated and our room was great--- even had a view of the sea! And the Naples restaurant was not closed but had a new manager and our lasagna the best I've ever had."

Now Selma and Frank were both urging her on.

"And your trip to the Vatican?' asked the beautician. 'That was the best part of the trip! Our tour group was chosen to have an audience with the Pope! He even talked to us individually. During our conversation, he asked me, 'Who did your horrid hairstyle?' ''

They hit the table and laughed so hard, the pudding dishes actually swayed a bit.

Marti was impressed with how united Selma and her husband appeared and appreciated their ability to still see humor in life despite its difficulties.

"Oh, God," she prayed, "Help me to get through my situation! Help Alfredo come back soon."

During his Key West stay, Alfredo fished and reflected on the dock as the sun's rays danced on the water—a rainbow of deep violets and the yellow of cornhusk tails.

I will live my life as if it will continue until I'm eighty. I will play baseball, buy a home for my family, father lots of children, and enjoy my fishing, he thought. *It's unfair that I'm the only one who got rheumatic fever. We all had bad sore throats infected with strep, but none of the other kids got heart damage as the result.*

Then he remembered his two siblings who died shortly after birth: I guess I'm lucky to be one of the nine siblings who survived... I don't want to let down Marti. She has her own dreams. Her aunt told her not to marry me. 'A hospital bed' she called me!'

He looked down at his swollen ankles, sighed, and threw his line violently. Then he spotted a passenger ship anchored in a distant Key West dock, a striking sight. The street appeared to end at the gangway of the passenger ship.

When Alfredo returned from Key West, the baggage handlers lost the suitcase with his pills, some of the many he would daily pop into his mouth. Once informed, the authorities insisted he sit in a wheelchair and enjoy a free dinner while they searched for his suitcase.

"Sometime later, every time I coughed the airport attendant assigned to me jumped straight from her chair. I did it a couple of times just to see her jump."

He returned to his highly paid fabric-dyeing job, thanks to Jimmy training him. Alfredo then collected both unemployment, disability insurance, and loans provided by Anna and Jimmy during his "spells."

"Marti, let's have kids. I miss a full house of children to play with," he said too loudly during a quiet dinner.

"I don't know... Let's wait for your heart to get better."

It would get better, though only for a while. The routine around his illness became second-nature in the household.

Marti felt it was better to postpone having children for a while. But things took a different turn.

8 DYEING
1934 - 1935

"Fabrics used to be made at home. The entire family would be involved in picking cotton or scraping wool from animals for thread."

"Yeah, Jimmy, I remember wanting to pick cotton and skinning our cows in Tampa."

"This was before you or I was born, Alfredo, at least four hundred years ago. In small Mongolian villages there are herders who'd skin the hairs off their animals, dye and weave them into yarn for clothing."

"God, I'd love to get back to living on a farm," Alfredo said as they stirred vats of dyeing cloth.

"Do you want to raise lambs for their wool?" Jimmy continued."

"No, I want to raise chickens and pigs, most. We could kill 'em for meat and sell eggs. You know, with this hard Depression, people want to buy locally."

"You would have to compete with local farmers."

"Okay, Jimmy, I've thought about that and plan to buy a station wagon, so we could sell door to door to our friends and the club members. There are lots of Spanish people living outside of the City also. Starting slow is the key."

"Your ideas are good, Alfredo. Yes, we sure do know a lot of people in factories. Gettin' back to what I was saying, guess where the dyes come from?"

"Plantains?"

"Close." Jimmy expected that type of answer from him. "The dyes come from plants and minerals, and even shellfish," he had to contain his laughter.

"Shellfish? How can dye come from a clam?"

"Not clams, Alfredo, a type of shellfish that makes purple dye."

"Sounds fishy and smells fishy also." Alfredo cracked himself up.

"Also, dyes come from plants. From the indigo plant we get indigo blue dye and saffron yields a yellow color."

"You mean saffron is used for dyeing clothes?"

"Yes, the saffron which yellows our rice can yellow fabric. But it takes much work to remove the saffron from the top of flowers. And now there are more chemical dyes used, so be careful to wear gloves."

"Why do I have to know all this, Jimmy?"

"Dying requires an understanding of dyes... chemical reactions, and fabrics. Y'know why the dyes are stored in porcelain containers?"

"No."

"Because they are very caustic and will stain and destroy other containers. You wash the containers with one part sodium dichromate and ten parts sulfuric acid. You have to know about these chemicals."

"Right you are. Well, I noticed how one of my fingertips fell off when I dipped it in."

"Okay, Alfredo, okay, you get the point. That is why test pieces of yarn are hung from glass rods and dipped into the dye solutions. If the color is right, bolts of fabric are dyed. Be very careful, okay, you don't spill any chemicals on your hands... or clothing." Masks were not worn at that time. Despite his warning, Jimmy did not realize the fumes entered through the respiratory system.

"Remember--- 40:1. It's the amount of water to dye for wool. Got it? And don't pack the test pieces tightly into the dye machines, right?"

"Is this the way you rinse off the fabric pieces?"

"Sure thing, here's how. Use two to five gallons of water for each pound. Remember to never change the order of steps when you get the right shade. Wet all the fabric and work it around well with this pole. With me so far? Okay, get the water out in that machine. Dry the fabric like this or you could ruin a bolt of fabric. You don't want that."

Jimmy laughed, of course, when Alfredo said he was going to melt into a toothpick in all this heat. Even the slanted windows in the twenty-foot ceiling, opened by chains, couldn't suck out the steam vapor.

"Sure, Alfredo, it is steamy, but if the dye is *too* cold it may break the threads. Right, wool fabric can be dyed directly. But silk requires skeins of yarn that you wind into these bobbins."

Alfredo caught on quickly. Six months later he was given the responsibility of supervising other dyers when Jimmy was out.

"Read this, Alfredo." A week later, Jimmy handed him a small mustard-colored book, *Constitution of Bleachers, Dyers, Finishers and Printers, Affiliated with the Textile Workers Union of America.* Alfredo read every word, cover to cover.

The jurisdiction of this local union shall embrace all workers employed in and about places of business engaged ... he read deliberately slow, as Marti brushed her teeth in the bathroom.

"Come to bed, Alfredo."

"... in the dyeing, finishing, printing, screen making, hand painting, and bleaching of all textile fabrics."

"Come to bed." She drew the covers back.

"I could learn all about dyeing and supervise all the departments, so even if I am out ill, I would have more job security."

"Alfredo, Jimmy and Pascule would never ask you to leave your job 'cause of your heart. Come to bed!"

"The union would also protect me. It says right here that they *increase job security.* Look for yourself—"

"Come to bed. I'll keep you warm and secure," she said teasingly, tossing her panties at him.

Alfredo worked for the next eighteen years. He learned to fill his palm with many pills and swallow them with just one gulp of water.

9 SCHOFIE
1600s - 1700s

Gertrudis, Alfredo's mother, was born and raised in Cuba, as was her family. For as long as they could remember, a great-great-grandfather, Emilio, spoke of his father, Schofie, a slave forcibly shipped over from Portugal. He served as a blacksmith, caring for the horses of a Portuguese import official who went to Cuba on business. Emilio remembered his father's story in the late 1600s. He was kidnapped while tending the family goats and taken to Portugal. During his journey, Schofie was told by an African guard speaking his dialect, "You will earn a lot of wealth and return to care for your parents before they reach old age."

"So why are our hands tied?" Schofie asked. He then spent the next fifteen minutes stemming the trickle of blood from the laceration above his eyebrow where the log had struck him. So much then for "returning" anywhere.

In Portugal Schofie learned enough of the language to understand that he was a slave. He grew reluctant to run away when he heard of African men losing their lives while doing so. The courts did not intervene on behalf of those seeking justice. He quietly accumulated money when his overseer was not around, selling horseshoes. He constantly worried about who would help harvest the crops with his father. His siblings were young, so who would carry the slaughtered goats to the market and negotiate for fair exchanges? Who would cut the vines so his mother could string baskets? Who would carry the wood needed for cooking? And who would participate in council village meetings, where his gift of problem solving was hearkened?

Eighteen-year-old Schofie was a chestnut-colored hombre with a distinct gap between his front teeth, always visible as he smiled often during his conversations with anyone who had an interesting story to share. He became drinking friends with a French sailor who would stop by a Havana port tavern every few months.

"I want to go home some day." Schofie's words stung.

"You could pay for freedom and come with us to Africa," replied the sailor.

Schofie told him it was not so easy. "There are few who know how to work metal the way I do." He thought about how lucky he was not to have been sold as a field hand. He heard they were beaten during the "seasoning process," rendering the slave to afraid to flee.

"What do you haul?"

"The usual, sugar and tobacco," the sailor said, putting aside a glass of honey-colored rum.

When Schofie had pulled together enough money to flee, the French sailor helped him by paying off the captain of a galleon who was preparing to sail to Mexico where a transfer could be made. Schofie slept on the gun deck in an Amerindian hammock. On the orlop deck and below were small barrels of fresh water and provisions. Unable to keep anything in his stomach, his first night was difficult. When he felt better, he had long conversations with Portuguese crewmen, who told him the owner of the galleon was a "flibustier" and had amassed great wealth.

Schofie figured this meant he was involved in a type of transport business, until the day the ship was attacked.

"Pirates!"

"Schofie, hold the ropes on this mast!" a crewman called out.

He did as he was told, his face slapped by torrents of water while praying the entire time, African prayers learned as a child. He shut his eyes as cannon fire filled the air.

Even at twenty, this was too much of an adventure for this mild-mannered young man. The cannons finally ceased. They had escaped *la muerte.*

Removing his soaked shirt Schofie yelled, "They couldn't steal our cargo!"

"Yes, they could not steal it back!" returned a crewman.

"Steal it back? Does the cargo not belong to this ship?"

"No, we stole it from *them.* That's how it goes in this business!" the Frenchman rang out.

"I see, I see, so the owner of this ship is a pirate?"

"*Oui,* a 'flibustier!'"

Schofie decided to stay for one year on the boat to accumulate more money. He was able to visit his family once and found his cousins were helping his parents.

His father knew---from the way his son's eyes brightened when he described Cuba--- that Schofie's return would not be permanent.

Schofie hid in a remote area of Cuba when he got back, since slavery remained alive until the mid-1800s. With the money he earned from three trips to Mexico, he traveled back to Santi Espritus, making connections with a group of villagers. Many had escaped political strife. They introduced him into their way of life. Schofie liked the discipline and policies of the villagers, even though the leaders dealt harsh punishment for desertion in battle. He soon wore African amulets and practiced Santería, an ancient religion which originated from the Yoruban people of what is now present-day Nigeria. When brought to Cuba, it soon was blended with Christianity to remain alive. He remembered how to lay animal traps and raise crops. But he and the villagers were in danger from invading Spanish soldiers, moving frequently to nearby villages. His blacksmith skills came in handy after he purchased documents from a freeman who had died. He opened a small shop catering to horses that were stolen from sleeping Spanish soldiers. Asked why they stole from the Spaniards, a leader smugly replied, "Look, they stole from us. We steal guns and horses from them."

Five years passed. Schofie purchased a plot of land. He befriended an Amerindian who moved after Spanish soldiers raided their village and set fire to their bohios, killing his young son. His friend's granddaughter, Eulalia, loved to tell stories and listened to Schofie's with delight.

She shared tales of her family who came from the southern region of Central America near the Orinoco river tributary. Her great uncle was a cacique during the early fourteenth century. Her grandfather disagreed with his brother over certain policies. Arguments lead to mistrust. Her grandfather had visited Havana regarding mutual fishing trade agreements. He retired from his position and brought his wife and four children to live in Havana. They left soon after the Spainards arrived

Schofie and Eulalia married. She bore him five children—one married a young Spaniard from Andalusia who settled in Cuba to farm; and their son was Emilio, Gertrudis's great-great-grandfather. Schofie opened a blacksmith shop in town as more Cubans settled in the area, and hired hands to work his farm. Even though some men of color did, he would not buy a slave. Never.

10 GERTRUDIS AND CHRISTOPHER
1895 - 1911

Gertrudis was born in the San Antonio de los Baños section of the outskirts of Havana Province. Sixteen in 1895, she was visiting a cousin to help care for her newborn in the city of Havana. She had bronze skin, fine features, and wavy hair that slipped onto her shoulders. Evangelista's father had emigrated from Andalusia and worked as a butcher in his cousin's bodega. He came from a family who made their living raising horses and livestock. He loved to ride horses as the men in the family had done for over a thousand years.

Gertrudis went to the meat market one day to purchase ground beef for picadillo, made with an onion, garlic, green pepper, cumin, a piece of ham, raisins, and tomatoes.

"Media libra," Gertrudis requested, pointing to the ham hanging on a hook. Christopher, the short Andalusia butcher replied, *"Media libra, para la guapa,"* (the good looking lady). They would marry and open a small bodega where the tocinos (cured sausages) hung above their heads. Stalls filled with thick malanga, yautia, yucca, and platanos surrounded them during their twelve-hour days.

Christopher, like many moderately conservative Spaniards, sided with Spain. Several of the customers spoke of the rural people living on the outskirts of the city, forced there by the Spaniard, General Weyler. Weyler felt that those living in the country were supplying food and shelter to the insurgents. He ordered crops destroyed, and livestock either destroyed or transported into the cities. The insurgents prohibited the movement of livestock. The relocated peasants became malnourished.

A customer buying two ounces of ham spit out, "You should see the thin children, Christopher!"

"The veguero's tobacco crops are burnt," muttered another

customer. "The price of cigars keep goin' up!"

"Why are there so few vegetables and so expensive?" quietly complained a third customer.

"Because of the war... My sugar and tobacco prices have risen thirty percent. This war will soon be over." He returned to smelling an avocado to assess its ripeness.

The war lingered. Currency was recklessly printed. In 1897, several Spaniards in town complained about having to do business with depreciated currency as payment for goods and services. Some were arrested and imprisoned, others deported. The war ended in 1898.

Christopher knew that many Spaniards had monopolized the better positions in Cuba and became owners of large tracts of land, secured government and finance positions, or were small shopkeepers. Those in the government protected the *Peninsulares* who practiced *sobrinismo,* bringing nephews from Spain to work in Cuba.

Christopher sat his wife down, saying, *"Mira,* Gertrudis, we must leave. Rebels from the countryside will take over this city and make it difficult for me." He did not support the Cuban-born Creoles who fought against Spain's domination. He was a *Peninsular,* a Cuban born in Spain. A proud, stubborn man. Tens of thousands of the rural people forced to move had died of diseases.

Some Spaniards had begun to leave for Europe, Latin America, and the United States, even though many Spaniards did support José Martí and the "Bronze Titan," Antonio Maceo.

"There are many Cubans living in Key West, and I hear the pay is good. Besides, a soldier from the Cuban Liberation Army opened a bodega across the street, and the *Criollos* will shop there."

"Pero, my family are here," Gertrudis protested.

Alfredo touched her hand and smiled warmly. "We will make a big family and visit Cuba. Florida is close by." After several years, his argument prevailed.

They settled in Key West with their first child, Evangelista, then moved to Tampa. His employer moved his cigar business because of the city's population growth, along with less union unrest. Tampa had a population of a little over one thousand people in 1895. By the time Christopher arrived in 1903, there were five to six thousand residents, a railroad, and a shipping line. He was a short, stout man, who loved recounting the macho stories of lassoing the most independent horses in Spain. He sat at the head of the dinner table with his nine children, all submitting to his steel-like stares.

They moved into a two-story wooden house designed for two families. Some buildings had balconies with Spanish-style ornate wrought iron. Gertrudis was responsible for the children's education. Shopping with a growing number of children came in handy. One child would run to the store with the stone oven for warm Cuban bread, another to Katz's store for household goods, and a third to the grocery store. Depending on their ages, the children played marbles, *palitos*, baseball, or softball with family members. However, the houses were so close that many more children came out to play.

Christopher quickly learned to support the cigar workers' union policy of hiring only Cubans. High salaries and decent working conditions were maintained, owning to the strikes. In order to survive as the newest arrivals, Cubans maintained their way of life. Only Italians, and not many, were allowed into the cigar industry. Cuban solidarity endured. But later, because of human divisiveness within the Cuban community, dominant cultures separated into service societies: the Asturians, Cubans, and Antonio Maceo, as well as Italian clubs.

Christopher's factory was made of sturdy brick. Wooden poles supported the overhead beams where lamps hung over the worktables. The workers' coats hung on the walls were a sort of decoration.

After the leaves were cured and slowly fermented, "so the leaf would die with grace" they were placed into bales, checked frequently "as a sleeping child," the foremen would say. When the leaves were ready, they were sorted into leaf grades by a selector who had trained for many years. Certain leaves were chopped under the crescent-shaped knives—*chavetas*—into filler tobacco, and then covered by longer leaves. The more expensive cigars had long leaves throughout, but there were many varieties and sizes. Once making the cigars was completed, they were placed into wooden harnesses and aged under constant maintained temperatures.

Factories often hired readers to help cigar rollers pass the time while performing their monotonous work. In this particular one, the readers sat on a platform four feet above the cigar workers. Sources of reading materials came from newspapers, novels, light soap operas, and political writings.

A committee of workers chose Cuban newspapers and titles by writers, such as Benito Pérez Galdós, Fyodor Dostoyevsky and Father Félix Varela y Morales, who wrote about culture and domination. The reader was highly paid. The workers' line of reasoning was *He brings knowledge; therefore, he is worth a substantial sum*. A man from the local restaurant traipsed around with two pots—one with boiled milk and the other with coffee—costly several pennies.

Years later, Christopher's granddaughter Norma, then forty, remembered the stories about life in the cigar factory when she attended the play *Anna in the Tropics* by Nilo Cruz, set in a Tampa factory and staring Jimmy Smits as the hired reader. The first time he appeared on stage, Smits's character was decked out in a white suit and tan Panama hat circled by a black band. The audience applauded roundly. The factory-reading committee asked him to read *Anna Karenina*, and he fell for a cigar worker---named, of course, Anna. And his lovemaking with Anna was *muy* sensual (on floor cushions in the factory). Anna confided to a friend, "He says dirty things to me during lovemaking." Norma imagined the words that he might have said and giggled. They were natural words of passion kept secret from young ladies and termed "dirty." This was particularly the case with her prudish mother, Marti.

The reader began at Christopher's factory, his white cotton shirt pressed perfectly and his brown pointed shoes polished and topped with tiny pin-tipped holes. During an emotional section of Galdós's *Fortunata y Jacinta*, the reader slung his jacket over the corner of a chair, as the workers' emotions began to boil. A hefty verbal disagreement ensued. The reader took off his thick bow tie and his words began to transform the cigar makers into a restless sea of mumbling, barking, approving, and disapproving waves. He adjusted his chair where his fedora balanced, and continued reading from Perez Galdós's *Fortunata Y Jacinta*:

Jacinta and Rafaela went upstairs. The maid was carrying a bundle of things, the lady's offerings to the needy in that severely poor neighborhood. Women came out, and moved by curiosity, the whispering started. And *soon*, in the murmuring circles that were forming, news and remarks went around: She's brought a lamb's wool cloak to Nicanora;---and a hat and a wool undershirt to Uncle Dido. She put five duros, like five suns, in Rosa's hand...She gave the crippled woman in number nine a blanket---and one of those flannel things to Señora Encarnacion. For her rheumatism...

Because of the voices, the reader stopped.

"She is not sincere!" one cigar wrapper said so loud that boisterous voices hushed her.

"She is too ... Just 'cause she has money does not mean that she is not a sincere person," shouted a man behind her. Others nodded while several pounded their agreement with their *chavetas*.

"Did the Spaniards who owned the sugar plantations care about the poor peasants and slaves who worked their lands?" someone called out.

"Not all plantation owners were the same! Some were sincere in providing for their workers," an indignant voice proclaimed.

"It's not about being 'sincere.' They--- as a whole--- did nothing to stop the slave importation. Nothing. But they did allow the condition of peasants to continue: no ownership of land, thrown off the land they had lived on for generations. Yes, the latifundia owners would attend silly balls in Havana while others suffered."

"Don't forget the miserable lack of education for the children!" thundered another from the back.

"Children with puffed- up bellies from worms --- no doctor to care for them, either," said a dark-skinned cigar filler followed by a chorus of *chavetas* hitting their worktables. So many people were talking at the same time! It was late. The reader pointedly put on his jacket to stop the conversation about the Galdós story until the next day, but the workers continued.

The discussion reached a boil when a woman accused a Spaniard of being under the illusion that his family was like the rich family in the novel. Of course, they both knew that only a handful were.

The woman straightened up. "Many of you were like the poor in the story written back in early 1800s!" she shouted.

"And many of you right here came without shoes on!" A muffled yell from a thin Cuban man chewing on the tip of a thick Cohiba.

A fistfight almost broke out between two overexcitable cigar workers who each claimed the other had been rude. A Spaniard claimed the passage in the book conveyed the manner in which only a small percentage of Spaniards in Madrid behaved.

"Yes, but these people grabbed wealth and turned their backs on the poor!" spoke up still another.

Christopher felt torn. After all, his birthplace was Andalusia. His father raised horses and pigs. They had been in a better financial position than those who lived in town, like the characters in Galdós's novels. He remembered too clearly the rags worn by children playing in the streets. His wife's cinnamon-hued color reminded him of the women in the Arab section of town, even though her family had lived in Cuba for centuries.

He grew weary of cigar making in his factory with decorative bricks around the windows, fire buckets filled with water near the entrance, and crowded workbenches. He was bone-tired tired of living in town with his growing family.

Christopher and Gertrudis talked of purchasing a farm, raising milking cows, with their abundant crop of children.

He attended events at the Spanish Club, which did not interest busy Gertrudis. After all, she suspected he also played the illegal *bolita* games. After dinner, he would bathe, put on a suit, and take the trolley downtown to the club until nine or ten. Gertrudis attended children's events at the Circulo Cubano.

All the Tampa clubs were mutual aid societies that provided children's education. This provided space for businesses, social, and political gatherings; medical needs, funeral services, and entertainment. *Zarzuelas* from Cuba and Spain with top- notch performers toured not only Tampa but also New York. The cigar community protected each other, Cubans, Sicilians, and Spaniards. They laughed at, or just ignored, the local American customs and laws involved with segregation; but this was not so in other parts of Florida.

Christopher left the J.C. Newman Company cigar factory when he purchased a forty-acre cow farm outside of town in order to sell milk and, mainly, raise his children. He and Gertrudis woke before daybreak. She boiled milk for the morning café con leche and buttered slices of bread. Chunks of cheese would be served or thick oatmeal. The boys milked the cows, which would stomp their hoofs irately if their nipples were pulled too hard.

"Careful...gently approach the nipple," Christopher would advise his sons. "This way, as if touching a woman's nipples, gently."

They poured milk, frothy with thick bubbles formed like a rushing stream, slowed by protruding rocks. The bottles were loaded into wooden crates and carried onto a wagon pulled by a horse. Each day, one of the oldest of the boys would travel twenty miles to deliver the milk to neighbors' porches, where wooden boxes were placed to receive the bottles. The barn had to be swept and the cows fed before the boys could walk one mile to school.

Gertrudis's anger peeked when the school official said, "You can't put that colored child in this school."

Christopher held her back and threatened to punch the school official for his stupidity. "Spanish Cubans are just as good as you." Gertrudis said. "I see how some of the other children get a poor education, but that's not going to happen to my children! Educated people of any color are treated with *respeto* in Cuba." The official relented, as fair-complexioned Evangelista was already in the school.

She remembered how her mother did not like attending the Andalusian Society Club events because she found them pretentious. Their emphasis, which amused Evangelista, was on Spain and Europe. The Spaniards often developed amnesia about their historical relationship with the Arabs, who mixed with them during their eight-hundred-year stay in Spain.

Gertrudis and Christopher lived to see all their children leave home, and they even traveled to New York City to settle down for a time with a daughter. But how they missed rural Tampa.

11 FRIENDS AND STORIES
1935

"Jimmy, you are not even listening," Anna said, annoyed that he was ten minutes late for lunch. She and Lola had planned to go shopping that afternoon. Time for such activities was rare because both of them worked overtime. Anna never complained, keenly aware of those who were completely without work during the Great Depression. She stayed fiercely independent. She had traveled to Morocco, Spain, and New York without her family, knew her shortcomings and would just not allow this man to dominate her now. Her independence and bossiness had become insulating fabric around her vulnerabilities. Jimmy appreciated her independence and hard work, but not her bossiness.

Anna did share Jimmy's resolve to live a good life. They were able to save most of Jimmy's salary by using her paycheck and the rents from three apartments, including the money to pay bills Marti and Alfredo brought in.

"Anna, not now." Jimmy waved her away and continued his heated conversation with Alfredo: "Joe Louis won because he's a smarter boxer!"

"No, he's stronger and quicker on his feet," replied Alfredo, immersed in the *Herald Tribune*. Looking up, he added, "Listen, Jimmy, all these important people—Reverend Powell, Duke Ellington, Ralph Bunche, and Mayor La Guardia—were in Yankee Stadium for the Carnera–Louis fight."

"About sixty thousand people showed up!" Jimmy said, pulling on his suspenders.

"Hey, that is enough arguing. Come to the table, *yo hice ropa vieja*," said Anna, cleaning her hands as the smell of *sofrito* filled the living room. "I paid twenty-five cents a pound at Ingoglias for this skirt steak."

The steak for rope vieja was cooked until tender and torn into slender shreds. It was sautéed in a fragrant combination of olive oil, onions, garlic, green peppers, cumin, oregano, tomatoes, and wine.

"I made enough for Ralph and his wife." The couple sat cozily in the living room, eyes glued to Jimmy and Alfredo.

Ralph and his wife were friends who were cultivated like special leaves of fine cigars. Mr. Rivas, a thirty-year-old mechanical engineer, supervised the factory dyeing machine repairmen where Jimmy worked. He and Jimmy had become instant friends after Jimmy asked him to examine the broken sewing machine in his home. He was five-foot-ten, broad shouldered, with a handsome face, resembling the people who populated Puerto Rico and the Dominican Republic. Mr. Rivas had rounded features and his straight dark hair was combed back, reminding Anna of the Cuban poet Nicolás Guillén. He had a boyish smile, always wore suits, and fancied his shirt collar secured with a bow tie.

"We should go on that bridge connecting Manhattan and New Jersey," he now suggested.

"Which bridge?" Jimmy asked, munching on a slice of green pepper. He enjoyed their crunchy texture, thinking back to the fresh peppers his mother would serve. She purchased them from farmers who filled roadside stands with rivers of vegetables in Italy. He would hear each farmer calling out to the passing people, "Come, picked this morning, the apricots—the biggest they've been in many years!"

"It was first called the Hudson River Bridge, but now it's the George Washington. It saves me fifty minutes to my New Jersey dry cleaners. You know, that bridge is the world's longest suspension bridge, about 4,500 feet long," Mr. Rivas said, deftly removing the sewing machine cover. Soon, he had the machine all fixed.

A few days later, Jimmy and Anna joined Mr. Rivas and his wife, Yesinia, in their 1930 four-door Chevrolet across the bridge. They stopped to marvel at the New York City landscape. Then they drove around Fort Lee, returning for dinner to 138th Street.

Mr. Rivas became a household fixture soon after Anna and Jimmy were aware that he lived in their neighborhood, right in the shadow of Mr. Rivas's alma mater, City College. During many weekend evenings, Jimmy, Alfredo, and Mr. Rivas could be found embroiled in a political conversation while they drank whiskey—or rum-filled shot glasses—and played gin rummy. "I like Roosevelt's idea of putting people back to work for the government," said Mr. Rivas. "You know, even photographers are being hired."

"Oh? Why photographers?" Alfredo held his cards close to his face.

"They take photos of everybody; the unemployed and their families. Later on… all will remember what a lousy time this was," offered Mr. Rivas.

"I must've passed ten men selling apples on the street on my way to work."

"It's even worse out West," Jimmy joined in. "Some people thought they would make a good living raising grass-fed cattle until the storms took over— rained for days. When it dried, layers of dust remained. The heavy winds blew the dust into blankets of clouds. Planting is impossible now."

"Mr. Rivas had to chip in, "Yeah, I do remember those rainstorms in the Dominican Republic. The rain and wind tore down most of the town's buildings and the sea claimed its share. My father was an accountant at a shoe factory at the time, and it took several weeks to reopen it." "Alfredo was holding onto three sixes. "My God, were you flooded from the sea?!?"

"No, the roads were shut down—impassable due to wind damage to bridges. The workers had to chase after their panicked horses too."

"Gin rummy!" emoted Jimmy, slapping his cards flat onto the table as Alfredo strained to look at Mr. Rivas's cards.

"It's too late to cheat, Alfredo. He won."

"I… cheat? If there is a cheater here, it is you!" A light glimmer in Alfredo's eyes.

"Mr. Rivas, you also play cards well… too well," said Jimmy, grinning slyly at this bear of a man, and giving him another thumbs-up.

"*Sí*, when I came to New York, I worked my way through college at the Grand Central Terminal cleaning the floors at night. The men would play cards at lunchtime. Once, I was given a five-dollar tip for helping a group of travelers who could not find a porter to carry their bags from the train to a waiting car. I was comin' back from a game, and I noticed these people with many bags looking for help. I heard the man call one of the women 'Consuelo' and stopped right in my tracks when I spotted this beautiful woman with a long neck. I asked her in Spanish if I could help with the bags. Later, I found out from a ticket agent that it was Consuelo Yznaga. And the other lady? She was with the wife of the grandson of one of the Vanderbilts, the family who owned all the trains that pass through Grand Central."

"She was a Puerto Rican?" Jimmy could not hide his amusement, chuckling during one of Mr. Rivas's too, too complicated stories.

"Nooo. Consuelo's father was a Cuban and Consuelo was a friend of the wife of one of the Vanderbilts. I got a five-dollar tip!"

"Did your family live here when you went to college?"

"That's right, Alfredo. My family traveled to the U.S. because of my father's new job as an accountant with the Puerto Rican merchant marines when I was ten. I learned English fast because if I didn't know the street names to get home from school, I would get lost in a neighborhood where the boys would try to jump me. I stayed late in school a lot because I didn't want to get beaten up outside after school let out. Some of the kids were gang members. I was the new 'pic' on the block."

"'Pic'? What's a 'pic'?" asked Jimmy, tapping his toe against the base of the table, anxious for Mr. Rivas to show his hand.

"What the Irish kids called me. Well, sir, later I learned the word was 'spic.' It took a while for me to figure out that was not a nice word."

"Well, I can remember a man calling me a 'ginny' and I said to him on a whim, 'No, I am Italian.'" A ripple of laughter from both men.

"Mr. Rivas, did your men finish repairing the dyer at our plant?" asked Jimmy.

"Don't know, I've been busy with my design project."

"I thought you only supervised, Mr. Rivas."

"I do supervise, and they call me if there's trouble on the job. You know that dry cleaning machines are double-barreled, one for the chemicals and the other for the clothes. Well, I'm working on improving the outer barrel filtration unit so more of the chemicals are reabsorbed early in the dry cleaning cycle."

Jimmy looked up after pouring a drink into his shot glass. "So, Mr. Rivas, you studied engineering?"

"Yes. It was called *technology* when the department opened in 1919. And I entered City College in 1920. That is where I got in the habit of wearing a tie, so the students would not mix me up with the gardener or kitchen staff. They'd see me as a wealthy Latin American."

"I know where you're comin' from. Y' know, some people assume I work as a butcher or in a fruit market."

"Jimmy I wanted to build and design machines, but it was difficult to find that type of work, y'know, the Depression. In 1927, I worked for an American company that sent me to construct electrical plants throughout the small towns in Puerto Rico and Santo Domingo. We stayed until 1931 and when we returned—me without a job—then the Depression hit. Boom! Like that!"

"At least you don't have to sell apples, Mr. Rivas."

"I do not want to take work from you, Alfredo." Mr. Rivas was holding his laughter in like gas in a beer can.

"I hear you don't take off your tie when you put on your pajamas," said Alfredo, as once more, Jimmy held back his laughter.

"You are a true rummy."

"What is 'rummy?'" asked Alfredo.

"A drunkard," Mr. Rivas slurring the words like he was one himself.

"Go on with your story…"

"See, Jimmy, it took a while to find a position in this New

Jersey repair company. I would not settle for any low-paying work. Like some of the men did who had to take positions way below their education. Tell me, what did you study?

"Me? How to get away from my family who wanted me to become a priest after high school in Calabria." Their raucous laughter quivered the cards a bit.

Mr. Rivas loosened his bow tie, feeling very relaxed from the two shot glasses of whiskey. "Is that why you came to New York, Mr. Tavoli?"

"Many Italians left for a better life, but I wanted to see the world. My father worked in government. We lived in a city, my family, pleased to remain there. I was not. I was sent to a Catholic school, and my mother had this notion. Well, that I should become a priest, so I enlisted in the service, traveled to North Africa. A cousin of mine had gone to Albany, so I went to work there for a few years, but I liked New York."

Suddenly, Jimmy threw down three aces, three kings, and one seven, leaning back in his chair, grinning--- the whiskey warming his body.

"Tell us, did that earthquake touch your family in anyway?"

"You know 'bout that?" Jimmy was surprised by how much his friend did know.

"*Sí, como no*, my father spoke to many merchant marines." Mr. Rivas removed his bow tie, a sure sign that all hell would break loose in this game.

"That earthquake was under the sea between Sicily and Messina."

"How did so many people die?" Mr. Rivas asked.

"When an earthquake erupts under the sea, a huge wave hits land really bad. The 1908 earthquake caused the wave that damaged buildings, injured so many. Actually swept people into the sea. My cousin's wife lost her two cousins in Messina. A shame. We were not hit, but thousands were killed."

"*Mira, muchachos!*" heartily from Mr. Rivas, as he saw his card sequence unfold as if from a magician's slight-of-hand.

"I want to run a farm someday like my father did in Tampa," Alfredo said, puffing on his cigarette. He began to cough.

His heart, Jimmy thought. *Alfredo should stop smoking. Now.*

"Sure, you could raise chickens in the back of this brownstone, but you would have to keep your roosters inside so they won't wake the neighbors," Mr. Rivas earnestly suggested.

"I had saved five hundred dollars toward buying a place outside of the City to raise chickens, but I lost it when the banks went under."

"Let's hope Roosevelt's ideas work. Then people will put their money in the bank to make 'em strong again."

"Rummy!" Jimmy burst out, laying down four Jacks.

In a few minutes Mr. Rivas would share how he met his wife.

Petite Yesinia had thick black hair, an oval face with dark raccoon eyes, a round nose, lips that puckered naturally when she made a point with a throaty laugh that punctuated her comments.

As a child, the Dominican-born woman had moved to East 110th Street after her stepfather, who was a lawyer and ran a newspaper, published articles criticizing the government. Government officials asked him "to leave... or else." Mr. Rivas made a quick motion of cutting his throat.

Jimmy tilted his head to the side, pinching his eyes a little. "I understand. Go on…"

Mr. Rivas related how her father worked on East 116t Street as a consultant in a firm specializing in travel and tax preparation. She had graduated from a New York City high school, pursued by many young men, even though she resisted thinking it was absurd that women were expected to marry so young.

Mr. Rivas continued his wife's story. "I came along, and she agreed to wait... I was busy in college. We dated five years while she learned accounting, enjoyed her friends, danced, and visited museums and Broadway shows."

Yesinia found that Anna shared her passions. They attended many *zarzuelas* and Broadway shows all over Manhattan and the Bronx.

"Well . . . I never!" a prissy Caucasian -American woman standing in a theater line bristled upon overhearing Yesinia speak Spanish during a heated debate with Anna.

"Why don't you mind your own business, *Señora?*" Mrs. Rivas challenged the blustery woman, who immediately shrank inside her rabbit fur coat.

"*Que gran puta!*" Anna gladly pitched in. "These Americans think that only English should be spoken in New York."

Marti would have stayed quiet, but not Mrs. Rivas. She chatted extra loud until they entered the lobby.

"What an insecure person you are, probably learned from a parent," Mrs. Rivas wheezed to the lady as they entered the theater. "You think Broadway shows are for a certain class of people," she finished, as the woman, with shoulders slumped scurried away.

With thirteen million out of work during the Depression, resentment heightened. There were those who felt personally threatened by people who like them being able to afford tickets for Broadway shows.

This incident reminded Anna of a newspaper article about the thousands of Mexicans who were being encouraged to voluntarily move back to Mexico. Many were deported. Mrs. Rivas shrugged and laughed it off, but Anna sensed this reaction was her way of coping.

A week later, Anna heard loud knocks on her door, and there she was.... Yesinia.

"Come in, Yesinia, please. How is Mr. Rivas?" Anna noticed how her usual friendly grin was gone. In fact, her friend's raccoon eyes looked downright fierce.

"Anna, a man died in my building!" Yesinia sat down as if the chair was endowed to give her strength.

Marti listened to Mrs. Rivas, while continuing to iron. It would be impolite to jump into a conversation between the older women.

"I was sitting next to the window in the kitchen, drinking my coffee, when I heard people screaming, arguing. I tend to face the window in the morning. You know, since my building is constructed in a square with a courtyard on the ground floor. There is less light in the back of my apartment." Anna felt like telling her to forget these petty details. But she just couldn't bring herself to disrupt this distraught woman.

"As I looked out the window, I saw a sort of misshapen bundle fall. When I ran into the courtyard, there was a body with legs all twisted next to his arms."

"Oh! "

"Did he fall by accident, or did his wife throw him out?" Anna resisted smiling.

"Well, yes, he was arguing with his wife. They say he had become more mean recently and had been acting strangely."

"Yesinia, you mean he... just... jumped out of the window? No!"

"Yes, Anna, did I tell you? The window was opened, only a screen covering."

"Do I know him?"

"No, don't think so, were new tenants. His wife works at Horn & Hardart's on Thirty-fourth Street. He lost his job." Both women's heads shook like bobble-head dolls.

Anna thought over how they all worked: Jimmy dyeing fabric; Marti sewing insignias on military hats (a skill she learned at the boarding school); and Anna supervising tenant issues. She also had a side business at home twisting brilliantly colored nylon fabric over thin wires into daisies, roses, and other flowers, then wrapped at the bottom with green tape. A sight to behold, stretching see-through nylon over thin gold-colored wires shaped into leaves.

"*Estúpidos!*" Anna had yelled when she read the banks had failed. She was pleased that she had encouraged Jimmy to buy property so they could make extra money from rentals.

"Was he a sick man?"

"No, Anna. The man had three small children!...Oh, I wish I was back in the Dominican Republic."

"You think this is not happening there? In Cuba and other countries, they all suffer by the failing banks."

"I miss my village." Her raccoon eyes teared up.

Anna made coffee. Marti continued to iron.

Mr. Rivas rang the buzzer, entered, and ran right over to his wife. "I heard, Pussy Cat. You will be all right. Sure, I'll take you home to rest," his voice, gentle as a moth fluttering around in daylight.

12 CULTURAL REALITIES
1935

Tony watched in delight as Lola burst into the room, expecting she would soon tell a funny story.

"Anna!" Lola exploded, her face taunt like an angry fist.

"What happened?!"

"Anna, remember when we talked about how *loco* some Americans are?"

Still ironing and folding her laundry, Anna sat down, revealing circular garters below her knees, her toes enveloped in blue slippers. "Calm down, Lola."

"Carlos and I drove to the beach on Long Island and stopped for a hamburger. We noticed a restaurant parking lot filled with many cars, so we figured the food was good. I noticed right away how the people at the counter stared at us. At our table, we waited for the waitress. Anna, I tell you this, we waited ten minutes, and then a man who came in after us was given a menu—and we weren't!"

Anna held onto every word.

"Carlos waved to the waitress who was servicing the next table. She ignored him."

Anna asked why they didn't leave. "Those Americans did not want you in their restaurant. You know how some of them are."

"I said to Carlos, 'We gotta leave,' but he stood and walked right up to the waitress and asked for a menu. We do not serve your kind,' she said."

"'So you do not serve Cubans here?' Carlos shouted into her mean-looking face."

"'Damn Niggers!' we heard someone shout behind us, and I turned to look at the man who sat next to a woman. Anna, their faces were so twisted."

"'You white whore,' that woman said, staring straight at me."

"'I am a Puerto Rican, you stupid bitch!' I screamed back."

"'I don't care what you are. Get outta here. Your kind is not wanted!'"

"I felt so nauseated. I grabbed the table for support and stood up. Then the waitress screamed again, 'We don't serve your *kind* here!'"

Anna again: "Those sons of bitches!"

"Yeah, then Carlos screamed, 'Come to our island to get the sun you hate, you stupid woman!' He refused to move an inch!"

Anna leaned forward as Lola put up her hand.

"I'm not done: A tall man ran out from behind the counter and pushed Carlos. Carlos drew back his fist, but I grabbed his arm and told him--- in a quiet voice--- to calm him down, 'Carlos, they don't want us here. Let's go. *Por favor!*'"

"'We don't serve any of you spics here!'" he shouted."

"'Carlos, they only want *their* kind, white Americans. We're outta here! Let's go!' They were looking at us with disgusted faces, like two skunks among them."

"So what happened, Lola? Go on, go on..."

I grabbed Carlos by his arm again and pulled him away. He held my hand so hard it hurt and pulled me out of the door. "We should call the police, Lola."

"But the police will side with them", I said to him. "In this country, there are laws that say people can serve who they want in restaurants. In the South, you wouldn't even be able to drink from a 'White Only' water fountain. This is not Puerto Rico. This is how it is in America. You know that."

Tony suddenly stood up. "I grew up in Tampa with some of those types. Some prejudiced people called me awful names' cause I was darker than them, even jumped me a couple of times when I was walking home from school."

Now Lola was on her feet. "Is that why you came here?"

"No. There are people like that here too, less obvious though. I feel sorry for 'em because they will never know us. Their loss."

"*Sí*, but I never saw this all the years I've lived here."

"That's because you stay in the City."

"Si, Tony, many Americans of color have told me about this ignorance."

"How dare these people --- immigrants themselves ---who came here so poor or badly treated in their own countries, do this to other people?"

"So, did you go home?"

"No, Tony, I begged Carlos, getting into our car, 'Please let's go home!'"

"'No! We're going to the beach, Lola!' he yelled.

"We drove to the beach and had a nice time, although we noticed some Americans ogling us." Lola said. When she smelled fabric burning, she asked Anna to watch the ironing.

"Something like that happened to my Filipino friend and my other friends of color... That is how some people are," said Anna with a resigned voice.

Lola shook her head. "Unfortunately, there is some type of prejudices everywhere. It is up to laws to control their expressing this to others. The laws of this county boost this kind of behavior...well, maybe they won't fifty years from now."

"Mrs. Roosevelt is not like them."

"Maybe so, Lola, but there are still those, y' know, who hang people in this country. Then those godless souls who watch and laugh. Two Italians were lynched by the local white people in Tampa 'cause they thought they injured some white woman in a cigar factory during a strike. Anna was surprised by Lola's denial, when she said," 'Tony, they don't lynch people in Puerto Rico.'"

"No, Lola they just let 'em die of sickness, with no doctors to care for them.

"*Mira*, Lola. There are white Spanish people in both Cuba and Puerto Rico who also are prejudiced. Some of these people just don't give a damn for people especially if they are poor."

"Come on, Anna, Carlos was respected in Cuba because he is a good businessman and a good person. People know him!"

"That is not the point, Lola. Poor or not --- businessman or not--- there are *mal criados*, poorly raised people--- in Cuba or here. Listen, even among the colored Americans, I see how in the movies and onstage at clubs, what happens. Whiter-looking performers are hired over those with darker skin tones. They are even discriminating against their own people. *Ay, que lastima!* Yes, a shame!"

"Bigoted, that's just how some people are Anna. But, also depends on how and where they were raised, and if the laws support this type of behavior," put in Tony. Lola held back talking as Anna began to fold her laundry. Then Tony laughed out aloud. Lola thought how strange this was.

"Lola, in Tampa there was a story written in a local white newspaper that said 'even Negroid people' had come to work at the cigar factories. The article was written just before the yearly Cuban parade celebrating Cuban independence from Spain. So two very dark-skinned Cuban girls were chosen to ride the lead float in the parade to show the Whites that we are proud of all our people."

"The Bible said God made us all in his image. Okay, but people don't act like they believe him," Lola said, throwing up her hands.

"Lola, they should act like us. We are too perfect for these imperfect people." Lola laughed.

"I agree with that Tony. Some people behave as the devil and should be made to kiss the asses of the Pope and his associates." She and Anna giggled.

The next week Jimmy walked into the kitchen holding an Italian newspaper. "*Anna, mira*," his finger pointing to one of the articles. "See this? Negroes threatened the King Julius General Market at Lenox Avenue and Sal Apuzzo's butcher shop because they're angry over the Italians fighting in Ethiopia."

"Is Ethiopia near Morocco?"

"Yes, in the north of Africa."

"*Estúpidos*," she said, finishing the story and returning to doing the dishes. "*Sí, estúpidos*," echoed Jimmy. "Anna, remember, I was in the Italian army during the guerra contra Libya. Italy dropped a bomb from a plane on the Turks in Libya."

"Tell me, were the Turks in Libya?"

"The Turks? They had control of Libya, so we fought against them to gain control of Libya. Many were injured. Now the Italians also want Abyssinia." Anna looked puzzled.

"I thought you said Ethiopia?"

"I did. Ethiopia and Abyssinia are the same country."

"Well, anyway, you're here safe with me," Anna continued to smile as Jimmy frowned.

"The Italians should stay in Italy." she said. "More injuries and deaths."

Jimmy returned to his chair, throwing the newspaper onto the floor. "*Anna, por favor*, bring me a cup of coffee."

The following week Lola dashed into Anna's apartment. So excited, she hung up her hat quickly and handed Anna two tickets. "You won't believe what I just got!"

"Lola, what a scare!" Anna said, meeting the "intruder" face to face and then falling back into her armchair. She noticed now another one of Lola's creative outfits: a satin gray skirt, a black tank top that revealed her bouncing breasts, and gold-colored sandals. Her hair, dyed pitch black, was cut in a Carol Lombard wavy bob.

"Hey, sorry, but look!" Lola waved two tickets in front of her friend. "Tickets to that *zarzuela* everyone is talkin' about."

"The show on 183rd Street--- with the singer Amalia Batista?"

Todo los Negros tomamos café, Lola sang, as she namboed around the kitchen table.

"How?"

"I mentioned the show to a customer last week. She came in to the salon today and said she knew the director."

"Is Carlos goin' ?"

"No. Carlos will be on his way to Cuba to see his mother. This is for you! Can you come, Anna?"

"Yes, yes, of course! Fulcida Montaner is really coming from Cuba to sing?"

"Of course!"

Anna wiped her hands on the apron that covered her floral house dress. "I read, I think in 1927, that she sang 'Ay, Mama Inez' next to a live horse, dressed in tight pants, boots, and a jacket like a coachman."

"No! You're joking?!"

"At the Teatro Regina in Havana."

"No!"

"And," Anna slowed down, seeing Lola's eyes open wide, "she was in blackface."

"Blackface? What's that?'

"She smeared black cream all over her face and painted her lips white, like in the American vaudeville."

"I don't think so, Anna."

"Lola, you sound like a Puerto Rico owl ... nooo, nooo," Anna mimicked giddily.

"Well, did she perform in blackface because of the American performers who do so?" asked Lola.

"I don't know. Why did she wear a man's outfit?" Anna lowered her voice. "Does Montaner like girls, not men?"

"No, she's married. She thinks women can wear pants like men."

"Lola, I think she wants her fans to know that many Cuban women work like men sewing, caring for children and making cigars."

"Okay, just that men do not take care of children."

"Yes, but, Lola, listen. Women--- as do men--- wear suits and make cigars."

"Lola, listen to yourself my friend, you know that women seldom put the cigars together. Only men do that. It's tough to choose all the types of leaves that make the filler, inner leaves, outer leaves, and wrapper. We mainly place the cigars in the pressers, put on the bands, or pack the boxes. But, *mira*, women could learn to make the tobacco selections too, if influential men would let us."

"You sound as though *you* worked in a cigar factory," Lola said. Did she just learn something new about Anna? She did not know her friend had been working since she was fifteen.

"My father grew tobacco on his small farm. He leased his property later and worked as a railroad supervisor... I went over to the cigar factories that purchased his tobacco."

"Anna, there was a Puerto Rican woman who was a lector in a Tampa cigar factory who wore men's clothing--- even a panama hat."

"Yes, Evangelista worked in a factory with a woman lector reading to the cigar workers."

"Do you think she liked... women?"

"I don't think so, Lola."

"Even the Bible talks about 'man lying with man.' God, it was going on then, too."

"Not in *my* family." Then Anna remembered her mother's second cousin, Antonio, who never married and lived for many years with his border. Lola, in the meantime, recalled her cousin Pedro, who everyone knew was the lover of the postman. Lola and Anna traded smiling, knowing looks.

"I think I will wear my new hat to the *zarzuela*," resolved Anna, walking over to the closet and picking out a hat that suggested a forest green glengarry.

Lola could not contain her laughter. "Anna, it looks like what those people wear who play, what is it called,... bag ... bagpipes."

"It is unusual, but the color matches my green dress."

They talked about which shoes Lola would wear to the show.

Lola studied the tickets. "I've noticed recent *zarzuelas* are about the relationship between the white, black, Indios, and mulattos in Cuba. But also about the rich and poor."

"Well, now with Batista, the power behind the President, maybe things will get better."

"If he does not become a dictator. "We've had too many dictators." Lola added quickly, "What do you think, Anna?"

"After the wars for independence that Cubans fought, and all those corrupt Presidents, it would be a pity if a despotic dictator would arise again."

"Maybe he will help the poor people get their land back." Lola added.

13 THE EXCITEMENT DWINDLES
1936

Coming home one evening on Manhattan's upper Broadway, Alfredo noticed men walking by carrying furniture. *Someone is moving,* he thought---until he spied his favorite stained coffee table, the one embossed with the familiar scratches.

"Stop! You sons of bitches, that's my stuff, my furniture!"

The three men dropped their furniture, ran past the bodega, Harry's shoe repair shop, the newspaper stand, and passed by Sol's meat market They were almost hit by the trolley car as they sped across the street and disappeared. People milled around the pieces like they were meteorites hurled from the sky. Alfredo ran to his apartment to find the door latch broken. He sat on the stoop trying to catch his breath just as Anna and Jimmy sprinted down the stairs.

"Alfredo, is it your heart?" shouted Jimmy, almost tripping over his shoeless feet.

"No, my furniture! They broke into our apartment!"

"Llama la policia!" Anna screamed.

"Oh my God, did they hurt you?" a worried neighbor asked, coming closer, and before long there were a cacophony of concerned voices from neighbors.

I saw them--- three Spanish guys. I thought someone was movin' outta my building! They ran down there, across the street."

"I heard one say, 'Hurry, hurry, Russo's store was broken into last week.'"

"I thought someone was moving out of my building!"

"They ran down there, across the street!"

"Get Alfredo a glass of water... Man, he looks faint," Jimmy addressed everyone.

"No, he needs a shot of whiskey," a neighbor said.

Two police officers broke through the crowd. "What happened?"

"They robbed us!" a bunch of neighbors shouted almost in unison.

"No, *stupidos*, my son-in–law, Anna said, pointing to Alfredo, now sipping a yellowish liquid from a shot glass.

One cop took a written report from Alfredo, while the second walked the block, asking neighbors what they saw. After they left, the neighbors carried the furniture back into the first floor of the brownstone. Except for the coffee table. Its leg was broken at an odd angle, like an injured race horse.

Marta arrived home getting neighbors' reports about what happened. Alfredo was so short of breath, she called an ambulance. She was not too surprised that in between gulps of air he kept joking while the attendants measured his vital signs.

His condition stabilized, he returned home in a week, but the thieves were not found.

"Marti, burglary happens in cities," Alfredo tried to reassure her. But he had lost a week's pay. The seeds of anger and fear were planted deeply.

Months later, when they accompanied Mr. And Mrs. Rivas to the movies and while they waited on a line, a man cut in front of Marti, who almost lost her footing.

"Mister, please! That's my wife! Be respectful here!"

"You wanna do somethin' 'bout it," the man from the South drawled with reddened eyes. A partially hidden knife was visible as he drew back his jacket.

"Alfredo, let's go! There are police over there!" Marti said, pointing at the theater door. She felt her stomach turn as she clutched her purse.

"Hey, man," Mr. Rivas called out, running over to his friends. Alfredo grabbed his arm and whispered, "He has a knife." His heart was racing as the man with the knife turned toward Mr. Rivas. Mrs. Rivas latched onto her husband's hand.

"*Joven...* " began Mrs. Rivas, shaking her head.

"No, Mama, please..." Mr. Rivas pushed her arm back.

"He must be crazy to carry a knife! Maybe for protection against his wife! You need protection from your wife, I think, don't you!" Alfredo shouted.

A ripple of laughter from people nearby, and the man left. Marti rushed to Alfredo side, worrying that he would need to be hospitalized again. But instead, he led them into the movie lobby, his breathing normal, checking who was in back of him. Marti grabbed his hand again.

"Not yet... we came to see the *Pick Up* movie, and no thug is going to stop us. No way!"

"But I feel dizzy, Alfredo."

"Just rest your head on my shoulder." He said it gently. But he kept on surveying his surroundings in the movie house, as well as on the walk to the trolley. Marti pretended not to notice as they got on the trolley.

" Sure, some people have become troubled themselves because of the oppression against them in this country," Mrs. Rivas said.

"Well, it has been difficult for many of us in the islands, but we have had respect for one another," Mr. Rivas added. But she was really concerned about the violence here. It was easier to speak of "the other" than of your own.

"It's a good thing that thug did not come closer, or he would have had it!" Alfredo said in a feeble but funny George Raft imitation. "My father always said 'If he is bigger than you, wait until he turns around and, boom!, hit him in the back of the head with something like a plank!'

"Yeah, like an ensiform sword!" Mr. Rivas laughed out loud.

Alfredo drew back his head. "A what?"

"A sword with a pointed tip!"

"So much like the Spaniard conquistadores!" shouted Alfredo, jumping into the aisle with an attack stance, swinging an imaginary sword above his head. What Alfredo did not question was why Marti felt dizzy.

Returning to their apartment, Marti ran to the bathroom and vomited. She then quickly showered.

"Sorry, Alfredo, I'm a bundle of nerves with all of this."

"I feel a little nervous myself, Marti, but there 's something that I should ask you."

"What?"

"Why didn't you tell me Anna was your mother? It is true?"

Marti felt strangely relieved. "Yes, Alfredo... How did you find out?"

" From Evangeslista. Anna told her."

"Anna lied to Jimmy before I came to New York. Even though she finally told him the truth, he spun out the same retread story."

"How did you feel?"

"Terrible. I still feel angry at Anna... I do!"

"So I've noticed. Do you know anything about your father?"

"Some family acquaintance, but Anna refuses to talk about it."

"Probably that's why she hasn't visited Cuba since coming here. They can afford to travel."

"Yes, she is upset. No, really angry at her father who blamed only her."

"Come here *mi amor*," He wrapped his arms around her. "Your father is Jimmy, far as I'm concerned. A wonderful father."

Marti was revolted by the gossip that Evangelista spread and how she had always been against their marriage. A strong bout of nausea struck her again.

14 THE FAMILY GROWS
1936 - 1937

"Sit down, Alfredo…"

"Sure, let me take off my coat. What happened?"

"I'm pregnant."

Alfredo grinned, jumped up, and tried to lift her skirt. "Any… bulge here yet?"

"It'll take months to see. I probably won't show before June. You just want to inspect my you-know-what!"

"Oh, yes, I do want to inspect your 'you-know-what," and he playfully wrestled her onto the sofa.

Two months later, "Do you still feel sick?" Anna asked her daughter.

"Nauseous …only when I smell strong-scented food."

"Here, I'll make you a cup of chamomile tea."

Alfredo knocked on the door of his in-laws' apartment and marched straight into the foyer.

"Anna have you seen Marti?"

"She's drinking a cup of tea. Some nice flan?"

"Fine, thank you, Anna. How was your day?"

"… just came back from the flower shop. We are so busy with the holidays. Specializing in handmade roses, lilies, and carnations. Here, take a look at these bags that I had to bring to get all my work done."

Alfredo glimpsed through the bags of colored netlike material, varying thicknesses of wires, ribbons, and green tape. Twisted together, they formed artistic bouquets poked into thick Styrofoam bases.

"Miguel will stop by later to pick up the completed ones and wrap them at the store. Each one is different. People like this. Take off your coat, Alfredo. How you been feeling?"

"Fine," he said, annoyed at how often she and Jimmy asked that same question. He hadn't been hospitalized in nearly six months. When his heart let him know when it was beginning to fail, he would take a day or two from work to rest. He drank his medications but did not stop smoking--- despite the advice of his doctors. He thought that he was still better off than those with tuberculosis. They spent months in a sanatorium.

From the box Anna removed a golden flan sprinkled with nutmeg. She slid a knife around the edges of the pan. She grabbed a flat dish in her left hand, the flan in her right. Then like a magician, she squeezed the flat pan tightly against the other pan, quickly flipping the pan's contents onto the flat dish. Sitting perfectly in the pan was a breathtaking two-tone custard dripping with a caramelized sauce the colors of egg yolk on a rust-colored piece of silk. She cut a slice.

"It looks perfect, Anna." He admired how resourceful both Anna and Jimmy were. She ran their boarding house and worked making artificial flower bouquets at home, in addition to piecework sewing. Jimmy was now manager of the factory's silk-dyeing section with seven men working under him. All this he gratefully acknowledged, as millions of people were out of work, the Depression slogging on.

Alfredo looked lovingly at his wife, who proved to be as resourceful and frugal as Anna.

"This Depression is serious Alfredo," Marti said. "I want to work until the baby is born. We'll save money toward our own house."

Anna poured boiled water over coffee crystals into a cloth sack, the colador, and added milk and sugar.

"How was work today, Alfredo?"

"Good! The union rep had a meeting with us during lunch. He reassured me that I'd still have my job if... well, I had to take time off because of my heart."

"You are lucky. It would be difficult otherwise," she replied, with an arrow- sharp side-glance from Marti.

"Yes, but we made up our minds that city living is not for us," said Marti. Anna knew not to reply. In spite of Marti's love for the excitement of the City- even following the incidents with the furniture and at the movies at heart, she felt she was a country girl.

While walking downstairs to their apartment, Alfredo kissed her cheek.

"I know you don't feel well in the mornings. Stop working if the pregnancy bothers you."

"No, I don't want to raise my child in the City. We are country people, Alfredo. I love the *zarzuelas* and the club we belong to. But wherever we go, there will be clubs, and we could come into the City to see shows... and stay here for the night."

Alfredo thought that if they did move away, he would be more independent even if his in-laws helped them. The City was just too congested. He basked in the memory of the quiet dusks when he was fishing in Key West, walking on Tampa roads at night, and loving a stream trickling onto a still pool.

Marti worked steadily for the next seven months, despite having to squeeze into the trolley car with her huge middle. She liked to travel downtown, where she could gaze at the theater marquees and find out which stars were currently performing: Benny Goodman, Fred Astaire, Ella Fitzgerald, and Mae West. Her shop was in the garment industry, on Forty-First Street. The girls at work often exchanged stories about the *zarzuelas* they attended. The day would pass quickly, and then Marti would make her way home, ambling slowly on the way to the trolley. Thinking about the baby who moved within her. She assumed climbing from her trolley stop up the hill to her brownstone was good for her.

One month later, during a walk in Riverside Park alongside Alfredo, Marti felt a rush of water down her leg. "That's strange, I cannot hold in my pee anymore."

The water continued trickling, Marti soon realizing it was not pee. "Alfredo, the baby is coming," she whispered. "My baby ... is coming!" he shouted, walking a few feet away from her, then rushing back.

"Almost forgot you," he joshed. "Can you walk? Could the baby fall out of you?"

"No, Alfredo, it takes a few hours... I can make it home."

He gripped her forearm and told people passing by that they were having a baby. Marti of course, tried to hush him.

"I notice she's big, oy," one called out to them, a Jewish merchant selling hats and gloves from his cart.

"Alfredo, please stop. You're embarrassing me."

"Stay here. I'll tell Jimmy to drive us."

"Please, honey, don't forget my bag. Maybe I should go upstairs and bathe."

"Bathe? You took a bath this morning. *Estas loca, mujer!*"

Jimmy ran down the stairs. Anna followed, then Juan and Evangelista, all the way down the block. Two tenants opened their windows to look down at the commotion.

"Well, did you bathe?" asked Evangelista.

"You two are crazy! Who cares? Those nuns see hundreds of births!"

"Ssh---Alfredo, where's my suitcase?"

"Oh, yes, wait a minute." He returned soon with it.

"Alfredo, please calm down... your heart."

The Catholic hospital was a short drive. Marti kept on

apologizing that she was wetting the seat of Jimmy's car.

"It's alright, just hold that baby in until we arrive." Jimmy held back a little laugh.

The doors of the emergency room banged against the wall as Alfredo ran ahead to the desk and asked what to do. He came back to the car accompanied by a nurse, who efficiently helped Marti into a wheelchair. Once in the wheelchair, Marti felt a cramp that started from her spinal column and raced to her belly button.

This isn't so bad... she thought.

Only Alfredo was allowed in her hospital room after the nuns, covered in black habits, dressed Marti in a hospital gown and measured her blood pressure and temperature. Marti was shaved in between the cramps, which kept on increasing. Alfredo sensed that Marti was obviously very uncomfortable.

"Would you like me to get you a hot dog at the Horn & Hardart?" was the first thing he asked.

"No, let's change places. *You* have this baby."

"Sorry . . . my heart," he said, grinning sheepishly and pointing to his chest. Marti screamed as another wave of contractions shook her body. Alfredo grasped her hand, "Push."

"I am not opened enough, you fool!"

"How much do you have to open?"

"About this much," Marti said, making a circle with her hands.

" Hmm, that big. I hope you close up again."

"Alfredo! Of course, I will. Please ask the nuns for something for the pain!"

"You heard, Sister, y' think my wife could have some pain medicine?"

"We like to hold off with it until the real labor has begun."

"*Real* labor? She is not now in *real* labor?"

"No, it could take ten or more hours."

"I feel faint. Do you have a bed for *me?*"

He returned to Marti's hospital room and told her what the nun had said. She squeezed his hand, exhausted, her eyes closing. She groaned each time a contraction came. Eight hours later, a nun came in carrying a tray with a quart-sized can.

"Sorry, you have to leave. I'm going to give her an enema," the Sister announced.

"What?!? An enema? She went to the bathroom this morning!"

"This helps the baby move into the birth canal!" said the experienced nun, about fifty-five.

"But what happens if the baby falls into the toilet?"

"Dad, that does not happen. The enema will help your wife, so please, please let me do my work."

"Go, Alfredo, and come back later," Marti said, her head down.

"Please look again and see if she is opened enough,!" Alfredo pleaded.

"Stand back!" the sharp-tongued nun commanded. She pulled the curtains around the bed.

"She's only five centimeters. Now please leave!"

"I'll be right outside."

The enema dilated Marti to nine centimeters. It took another grueling hour to reach ten.

The words push, push, push is all Marti remembered of the next hour. Alfredo had left the room because he felt lightheaded and had the urge to punch the gruff nun in the mouth. Luckily, her tour was over and a younger, jolly nun came in, one who even joked when Alfredo asked for the hundredth time when the baby would come.

"Sir, when God wishes it, but He wishes us to rub your wife's aching back in between contractions, and for you to stay on your feet because if you faint, she may stop pushing."

When it was time, the nun rushed out of the hospital room, instructing the desk clerk to call the doctor.

When Marti was wheeled out into the corridor, Alfredo was strictly forbidden to follow her gurney.

Twenty minutes later, the nun carrying the baby faced Alfredo. "It's a girl!" she exclaimed in her Irish brogue. As Alfredo held his daughter, tears began to well up.

"Can I show her to the family? I promise not to take her home or leave the hospital to get a hot dog."

"No, wait until we clean her," the smiling nun said, lightening up a bit. "On the other hand, you could buy me one with ketchup and mustard if you go out."

Alfredo brought her two hot dogs later.

"Mira, what came out of me?" Marti stared amazed at the placenta: *It looks just like the roots of a tree ripped out of the ground.* Just then, Alfredo entered the delivery room and spotted for himself the placenta.

Marti repeated her placenta comparison. *"Tu estas loca!"* Alfredo let out a mock shriek, gazing in wonder at his bronze, thick-haired daughter.

"My grandmother... she looks just like her!"

15 A MOTHER'S LIFE
1937 – 1938

Mr. Rivas became Maria's *padrino,* her godfather. Later, his wife with the raccoon eyes helped care for Maria, joking with Marti about the effusive absurdities of life. She enjoyed her role as the experienced friend since she and her husband had two children. She appreciated Marti's formal and polite manner, like the women had in her country. She thought about how she hated coming to New York. She refused to learn English for a long time. She detested the noise and missed the sea, her girlfriends, and her favorite neighbor who warmed her heart with his daily poetry about people, flora, and fauna.

Marti stayed home from work. Alfredo wouldn't even discuss the possibility of her returning to the factory. She took the opportunity to carefully study the words and lyrics to Broadway shows and Spanish *zarzuelas* and Italian operas. She loved singing to Maria.

Maria was to become the most sensible, insightful, and wise of the children to follow. She received the patience and wisdom from her grandparents, the discipline from her mother, and the playfulness from her father. Jimmy would take her for long strolls from before she could remember. Once she was able to talk, Jimmy would ask how her day had been and encourage her to respond. She listened with the same kind of attention shared with his adult friends. Alfredo would sit her on his lap and read bedtime stories, becoming the voice of each character. Maria was swept along into vivid scenes of imagination like floating into the air under the umbrella of Mary Poppins with one of the children she cared for. Eeyore, her stuffed donkey, sprang to life in her room among her other stuffed animals.

Marti joined the Manhattanville Mother's Club, located above 120th Street, where classes geared to educating young mothers were conducted. Nearby, factory workers unloaded from horse-driven wagons large metal cans with New Jersey's fresh milk. It was poured into bottles, capped, and delivered to the wooden boxes that were set out on doorsteps.

Alfredo joined the New York Club Fraternal Regeneracion, started in 1930, opened mainly for Hispanic men. Cubans formed many associations in Cuba, Tampa, and New York. In earlier times the organizations were weapons against unfair political and social conditions. All segments of the population started clubs: labor, students, women, Catholics, and political organizations. In Cuba, plantation owners belonged to social clubs, free men formed loose-knit unions and so-called slaves had their mutual-aid societies. Some of these club members banded together in the late 1800s to fight Spanish domination and slavery.

With the dues that Club Regeneracion collected, loans were provided to members who were going through difficult times or needed to start a business. Alfredo's brother, Ramon, borrowed money to buy his first truck, and a second one two years later. His brother came from Tampa in 1934 and worked in the garment industry until he purchased his own delivery truck to haul bolts of fabric.

Months later, Marti was invited by the club's secretary, Mr. Rivas, to sing at a fundraiser. She was asked to accompany Marti to the exciting event.

Marti had asked Lola for clothing suggestions. Marti was frightened by Lola's choice of a black sequined dress, black matching hat with ostrich feather, black three-inch heels, and elbow-length nylon gloves. She was determined to choose her own outfit. Her husband and Alfredo went to the hall early to set up. When Mrs. Rivas arrived at Marti's apartment, she found her still in rollers, black hose, black slip, slippers, and surrounded by a pile of clothes.

"Nothing fits me, including the suit I just bought! I can't go tonight!" Marti sat sulking, her face stained with tears.

"You are trembling.... Let's find an outfit," Mrs. Rivas suggested, letting her fingers carefully glide through the clothes. "Have you tried this long black skirt?" she ventured, aiming Marti to the closet.

"No."

"Go ahead, try it on while I search for a blouse. . . See, this blouse here is lovely, and it matches this jacket."

"That's the blouse and jacket of the suit."

"Try 'em on over the long skirt."

Marti put on a frosty smile, feeling that maybe she did look presentable in the long skirt.

"You look great!" Mrs. Rivas's eyes brightened. Her throaty horse-like deep tone filled the room as Marti studied herself in the mirror.

"These opened-toe shoes match the outfit. Leave on the black sheer stockings." Mrs. Rivas advised.

"This skirt fits a little tight since the baby," Marti admitted after seeing the collar of the blouse forming soft waves around her face.

Mrs. Rivas felt her friend looked sweet, but also sexy. "It looks great, the skirt is tight enough to outline your fanny. Shoes now, come on.. Now to get her to change those earrings," she said softly as she could.

"Any gold- colored hoops?"

"Yes. These. But they're too big." Marti wobbled on unfamiliar high heels.

"They are *perfecto*. Now, let's put this linen white rose in your hair." She was hoping that Marti wouldn't start objecting.

"No, sorry, I look just like a trollop with it."

Mrs. Rivas didn't want to push it, afraid that if Marti did get into a snit, she might altogether reject the skirt and blouse.

"Yes, maybe it is too much," Mrs. Rivas agreed, throwing the rose back into the drawer. "But what about these gloves?" She pulled out long nylon black see-through ones, with frilly ridges.

"Yes, Lola suggested those. They fit fine. Well, what do you think?"

"Wonderful, time for your make-up. You do want to look the part of a singer."

Marti gave in.

"Even Mae West would bet you look like a movie star now."

Marti put on her coat while Mrs. Rivas positioned her hat like a badge with its diagonally attached feathered cordon.

"Come Around and See Me," sang a beaming Marti, hugging Mrs. Rivas. "Let's take a cab, like entertainers do, over to the club to meet with our husbands."

The wide glass doors of the fundraiser hall were like movie theater entrances. Escritoires and mirrors lined the hallway. The walls were decorated with fading flowered wallpaper. A ticket booth and coatroom housed shapely girls in green sequined tops. The next double doors led into a dimly lit cocktail lounge dotted with chairs hugging tables and a curved bar with stools filled with memories of their occupants' tales.

The ballroom, lit brightly by chandeliers, looked like an ornate movie theater, only without seats. The forty tables were bedecked with embroidered linen tablecloths provided by the members' wives.

When the women entered, Alfredo sauntered over and watched as Marti took off her coat. He smiled and extended his arm.

"Madam, may I escort you to your table?"

Marti cast a smile, a timid one, of her own. The tables and chairs were half- occupied. Those attending from the club's one hundred members had invited family and friends. Gold griseous wallpaper covered the walls and twenty-five egg-sized light bulbs glistened from a suspended chandelier. On the stage, fifteen musicians swayed, bounced, waved handkerchiefs, dusted their moistened brows, and vibed in unison, like a team of synchronized boat workers. A cha-cha began the set. People filled up the dance floor. A rumba next, then an equally fast-paced mambo. The walls were decorated with red, blue, and white crepe paper, which matched the patriotic-infused streamers dangling from the ceiling. The stage had four flags projecting from stands. They represented the US, Puerto Rico, The Dominican Republic, and Cuba. The islands were their homelands, although there were also Mexicans, Colombians, Spaniards, and sprinklings of other ethnic folks.

Three side tables were filled, all in good spirit, with competing dishes - stewed chicken with potatoes and peas; saffron rice that was as orange as the peas were green in the rice with chicken; arroz con gandules; various platano dishes with shades of pale salmon and metal rust; carne guisada dishes, pasteles wrapped in paper whose scars of string bindings remained; potato salad adorned with hard-boiled eggs, coleslaw, avocado slices decorating green salads; and the pernils whose crispy skin emitted steam.

The beverage and dessert tables were in a separate part of the room. Flans, sponge cakes and bread puddings were carefully prepared in order to show the abilities of the donor. The dulce de guava and white cheese slices were neatly placed onto crackers and piled onto a pyramid. Each woman had made her best dish. Metal buckets held ice. Bottles of rum, whiskey, gin, vodka, wines, and sodas lined the tables, creating a bottled miniature skyline interspersed with gardens of cut limes and lemons where they sat. From where the men sat, they would share the cost of "set-ups" for each of their tables: cups, ice, and one or more bottles.

The men wore crisp suits and fedora hats. Elegantly varied were their alligator, black patent leather, or brown suede and leather pointed shoes. The women, of all ages, wore glittering fantasia rhinestone jewelry, tight dresses with low neck lines. High heels pushed out their rear ends. The children wore their church clothes and knew--- by the sharp looks cast at them--- that they were not to pick up the liquor bottles. The bustling young dancers had to quickly sip from the cups before the hand of an adult would grab it from them. Not to mention parents shaking their children's bodies with delicate arm-twists. During the first band break, Marti was introduced to Pedro the bandleader, who agreed that "Lagrimas Negro" and "Siboney" would be fine. They played it loud enough for her to hear.

"I will cue you in between musical pauses, so watch me carefully" were Pedro's only instructions. Still nervous, Marti sang to herself practicing alone in the wings, waiting for her turn to go on.

At the end of the second set, the president of the club thanked everyone for empowering the successful fundraiser and introduced "Marti, our club member with the lovely voice."

But jittery Marti wished she hadn't consented to this. She looked slowly around the nearly filled tables. She found Lola and Mrs. Rivas, who were smiling and nodding their heads in approval. Lola's polka-dot dress with matching beret amused Marti, and she now felt more assured walking onto the stage as cheers erupted from her table. She made eye contact the band, which began the slow bolero. Marti began singing so softly that the band conductor signaled for the band to lower their sound. Closing her eyes, she envisioned being in her kitchen, where she sang all the time. As she formed this picture, her sound went up, and she remembered to watch the band leader. So she turned to his beaming face, relieved that she had not forgotten the lyrics. When the audience clapped, she heard Alfredo's weird whistles of delight. She sang the second number, more upbeat, after which the president came on stage and gave her an oversized hug. Marti's nylon black evening gloves and her coquettishly swaying hips became her signature, as she continued to sing publicly from that day forward. It was as if she were in her kitchen, joyously covering arias from *Madame Butterfly* and old Cuban love songs. Alfredo felt proud.

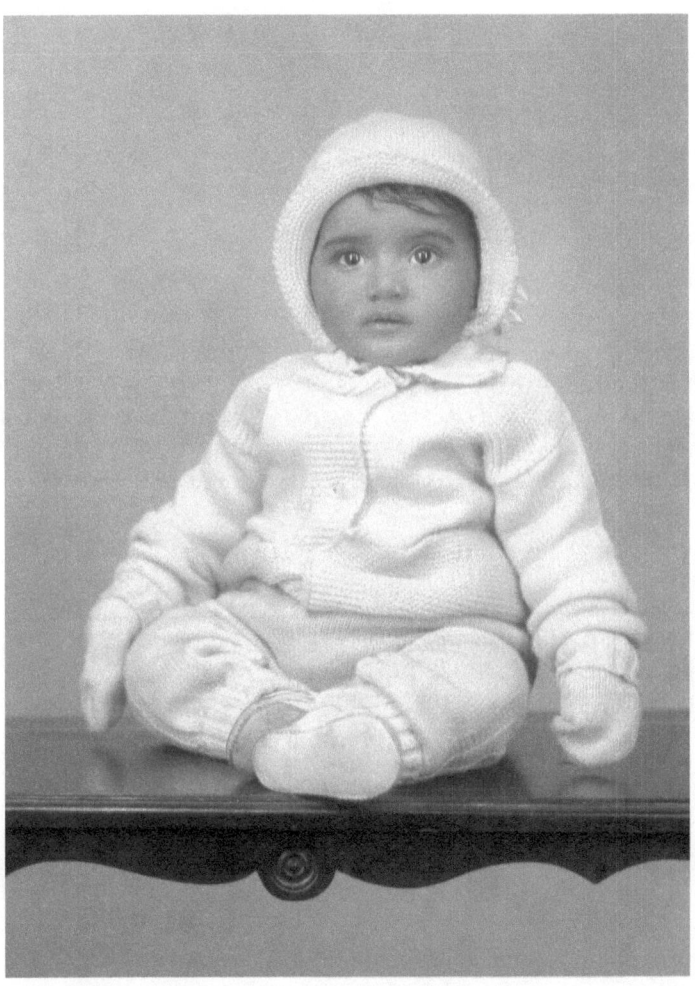

16 BEYOND THE FAMILY
1938 - 1939

Dear Marti,

How is Maria? Your great-aunt Graciela is well. I gave her fresh fish and she made paella for me … almost as good as yours.

We talked again about all of us visiting Cuba next year. Graciela has not been back since her brother's wedding. She said folks in Cuba understand that due to my illness we could not attend but wondered why your mother wasn't there. My brother Nick warns me that travel could become difficult if Hitler's threats continue.

The days are boring here without Maria, work, and, of course, you. Will come home soon.

Love,

Alfredo

Alfredo felt guilty, glum, and helpless at not being able to work. He made up for it by pushing himself hard to achieve some of his dreams. He would show his family--- and himself---that he was still capable.

Anna had interceded on behalf of her Aunt Graciela to help speed up her immigration to Florida. She planned to work for a Cuban family.

Anna, my immigration papers are as slow as a broked down cart. Graciela wrote. Immigration laws had slowed entrance from the Caribbean to the US to a dribble.

My husband agrees with me that another revolution in Cuba is possible if things don't change.

Graciela's husband had resisted the move, but now preferred to transfer to a US merchant marine company. There had been another strike of stevedores. He worked fewer hours then.

In Cuba, following the ejection of the Spanish government, unrest and assassinations persisted. Cuban fighters had been called by the United States press after this 1898 war "looters,

98

troublemakers, unfit for self-governing. "Yet by 1905, sixty percent of all rural property in Cuba was mainly owned by Americans who rushed into the war-torn country filled with widows. The rural population, in some areas, had been removed to the cities during the war. Corruption grew... as did population unrest. Government forces killed over one thousand members of the Independent Party of Color, which had requested political changes in 1912. Rising together in anger like a disturbed nest of hornets, were university students along with intellectuals, dissatisfied lower-ranking soldiers; and of course, workers in low-paying jobs.

Government forces came down on them hard as bulldozers. The people were tired of low wages, rural children dying of intestinal worm infestation; lack of health care and education for the poor; flagrant segregation by color, maintaining "tourist only" beaches, and of the profuse brothels and mafia-controlled casinos in Havana. The wives of local Cuban officials received mink jackets—in tropical Cuba—as bribes from organized criminals.

Those who fought against the status quo set fire to cane fields, assassinated officials, and leafleted the public with their demands. The captured protestors were jailed, tortured, and exiled. When released they went into hiding, many vowing to continue the resistance.

In 1933, President Dr. Grau San Martin promised a "new Cuba," manifesting women's suffrage, an eight-hour workday, and minimum wage for cane cutters. The military leader, Batista, who merely sat grandiosely by the sidelines, increased his power and later supported the Cuban oligarchy in the coup that overthrew Grau. Grau was later reelected, but then deposed by a coup lead by Batista, who cleverly sided with a popular workers' group and the Communist Party to win the presidential election. Batista did support Grau's promises to reduce social unrest, and political changes occurred--- but not enough for too many. The future would bring another revolution that would end in Fidel Castro's meteoric rise to power in 1959.

In the early 1930s, Graciela and her family were fearful. Their son, who attended the University of Havana, fell in with members of a student organization, the members of which were routinely arrested. Anna was busy with her boarding house business, using that as an excuse not to travel back to Cuba. Her father, who never wrote to her, had remarried and moved to another province. She was not ready, too proud, to meet again with family there who she dreaded, would still harshly judge her. She had calculated that if she did the right thing by paying her daughter's tuition, he would accept her. Her travels had opened her eyes to the human condition. Her father would not change. She did, however, want to help Graciela, who had solicited Anna's first au pair job. Anna did not know that Graciela thought of her as a hero because of Anna's world travels, her solo journey to New York as a young woman, and marrying a man of substance. In a way, she had broken the traditional chain of the male-dominated Cuban culture.

Anna used the Cuban method of directly asking someone in power for a favor. She sent a note to Carlito and his father, the Cuban UN diplomat--- her former employer--- requesting a meeting. She took the 86th Street trolley, toting a cloth shopping bag with a metal bread pan filled with a flan. She walked along the edge of Central Park, with its crisscross paths of sleigh marks. As she did, Anna observed that peoples' coats began to look more and more expensive. She patted her own fox- fur collar and straightened out her fox-lined hat, sensing how good she looked herself. She thought about her earlier journey to this neighborhood. She veered her eyes toward the doorman at the 88th Street brick apartment building. He recognized her face but couldn't remember from where.

"*Hola*, I'm Anna Tavoli. Don't you remember me? She asked the doorman. I used to work for the Cuban diplomat. He studied her face and touched his own, his mouth open a little.

"You look lovely. What are you doin' now?"

"I am married and own a brownstone near City College... I have an appointment here."

The doorman called upstairs to announce her visit, and lost in small talk, they walked together to the elevator. Anna noticed few changes in the narrow lobby that was dotted with ornately framed mirrors and straight back chairs. The brass elevator snapped to attention, its doors promptly opening to admit Anna.

She hugged her now grown former charge, handed him the flan, and Carlito, immediately invited her to sit down. They began a thirty-minute discussion about his recollections of their years together, particularly their fun -filled walks in Central Park, and then caught up with happenings since parting. When his father came home, Anna asked him to push forward her aunt's immigration papers. She stressed how the change in immigration laws had made it difficult for Cubans to emigrate. Anna felt right at home with Carlito's father. Her past experiences with wealthy families helped diminish shadowy fears. She understood that all walks of life have similar family dynamics and problems. While not overtly religious, Anna believed God had leveled the playing field for all.

Lola sat in her apartment that evening as Anna recounted the story. Anna's request was fulfilled several months later. She remained as brazen as ever.

That winter, Marti knew Anna would never go back to Cuba while her father was alive, so she planned to visit Cuba without her. Her plans changed. Marti thought back to the terrible call she got that Alfredo had passed out at work. His ankles were not even swollen. He said he felt dizzy, leaned against a wall, and slid to the ground. The doctor said not enough blood was going to his brain because his heart muscle was slowing down.

"You should consider not smoking. You work in a place with all those chemical fumes in the air," the doctor repeated, though feeling quite helpless. Alfredo needed surgery. His damaged valve cried out for replacement, but that kind of operation was still experimental and couldn't be performed safely yet on humans. The doctor increased the dosage of medication to strengthen the pumping of Alfredo's heart. He managed to recover in Key West and returned home. He looked forward to New York's fall foliage.

Then the news came suddenly. Germany had stormed into Poland, and their travel plans had to be curtailed. Thankfully,

Alfredo's episodes of shortness of breath and palpitations slowed down after new medications were added. He followed, at least partially, his doctor's recommendation to stop smoking altogether.

"Should we go to the World's Fair?" asked Alfredo, weeks later.

"It is expensive with Maria . . ." Marti had almost continued, but changed her mind after she saw her husband's disappointed look. "Of course! This fair happens very rarely -- not to be missed."

Realizing that he might not be alive for the next World's Fair, Alfredo on a daily basis used this philosophy of carpe diem to take advantage of what was before him.

Trolleys headed to Flushing, Queens, where the World's Fair was being held, were crowded with men dressed in colorful knotted ties: and women adorned with smart- circular brimmed hats. She and Alfredo trekked up a curved entranceway among hordes of people. Marti felt proud. Alfredo looked so handsome with his narrow moustache, suit, and fancy tie. He spent time studying the exhibitions that incredibly showed what New York would look like in the sixties, complete with trains speeding along at sixty-five miles an hour.

"Marti, look at the many lanes the roads have that lead out of the City to the farming areas. See the curved road edges, like racing tracks." Alfredo's burst of enthusiasm made her glow too. He reminded her of a fourteen-year-old cherishing his baseball card collection. "Fifty, seventy-five, even one hundred miles per hour the automobiles will travel!"

"We could get to a house in the country in less time!"

"The curved sides are for safety, Marti. There's a commuter train that already goes upstate."

"I could travel by train to the City!"

"That so, Alfredo? When it snows?"

"Probably could stay in bad weather with one of my sisters until the farm is all set and eventually work up there."

"Alfredo, this transportation system will move more people outside the City. More factories will open."

Alfredo added : "They will need milk. *our* milk...or chickens."

"But can we afford to buy a farm, Alfredo?"

"Yes sir, Tony, Ofelia and her husband said they would rent a room during their vacations."

"Tony can be our carpenter, Marti."

"Hey, you're thinking we should run a boarding house for people on vacation?"

"Yeah, maybe..."

"But your heart... ?" Such thinking was painful to Marti. She knew her husband still smoked (though he hid it!), drank rum, and played baseball hard in the park with his friends. But she also knew the periods he had to take off work to rest were decreasing.

"I met a man who was in his sixties with a rheumatic heart, and he's still working … you are too skeptical."

"No, I am practical."

"Yes, my dear wife, my own lovely bush among the landscape of shrubs, grasses, and bushes. But, I'm lucky that you are also *practical!*"

"Be serious…I want to leave the City, Alfredo. Even rich families are unable to protect their children in this country. I want to live away from many people. Remember what happened in the early thirties with the Lindbergh's baby?"

"You see, you worry too much," replied Alfredo, masking his own uneasiness. "Come on, there is a Cuba exhibition."

Back at their brownstone, Anna checked on Maria sleeping and joined Jimmy, who was reading the newspaper in the living room.

"Anna, we'll have to buy war bonds, if there is a war. The Nazis are evil. They will try and take Europe and come after us, if we let them," Jimmy said, flipping through his newspaper. "It would be a good idea for us to have some land in the country. In Italy, those with land did quite well during hard times... Alfredo wants to buy land, a farm he said."

"Do you really want to move outside of the City?"

"No. Anna, I like the City. I like my work, the shows, and all the friends we have here."

"Do you want to visit your family in Italy before the war gets worse?"

"Ever since my parents died, I have no wish to visit. But it was good to see my brother when he came here. Remember our neighbor, Esther?"

"Sí, la Judia."

"Her brother writes all the time about that hateful discrimination in Germany. She's trying to get him out, but there's a quota on the numbers who can emigrate."

"I read that four thousand Mexicans were deported from this country 'cause of the Depression. It is very political who is allowed here. And once here, many are pressured to leave," said Anna. She paused, then added, "America is lucky to have us. We work very hard, never asking for handouts even with the Depression. Right?"

"Yes, we are lucky. You have embroidery skills, and I can run those complex dyeing machines." Jimmy had heard about the many farmers and others out of work, so he added, "Yes...yes...I think it is a good idea to invest in property, perhaps with Alfredo.

"Yes, but it may be difficult to draw income from only land." Anna said.

"Jimmy, Alfredo is talkin' about buying a farm. Do you think with his health problems it's a good idea? Be honest."

"Maybe not for his heart Anna, but for his mind it is."

"But his mind is not sick."

"True, but Alfredo is highly spirited. Y'know, he wants to live life to its fullest, despite his illness. That's why he continues to live the way he does."

After returning from the World's Fair, Maria woke from a nap and ran over to sit on Alfredo's lap. He bubbled over, discussing their World's Fair adventure.

"Papa, are we gonna live somewhere else?"

"Maybe, Maria." He brushed her long hair away from her face surprised how insightful she was at barely four. This was partly so because Anna and Jimmy explained to Maria all the sights and sounds of their neighborhood. Jimmy answered all her questions: "Where does the sun go? Where does the milk come from that's left next to our door. Where?"

So often, they would sit together in the park watching the people stroll by the ice cream she was holding cone leaked onto her fingers.

With Maria on his lap, Alfredo would read her bedtime stories and explain how Mary Poppins could fly. Maria thought that Mary's umbrella had an airplane underneath it.

"Anna and I agree that owning land is a good idea. Top notch!" Jimmy concurred, but soon stopped the conversation. He did not want to raise hopes, in case their idea turned out to be only a dream. He was wrong.

17 SEARCHING
1938

Marti, Alfredo, Juan, his wife, and Anna squeezed into Jimmy's Chevy for a drive to upstate New York. They watched flowers of different shapes and sizes sway in costumes of startling colors along the roadside. They strolled along ponds that were dotted with lilies and chrisom leaves, guarded by velvety equisetums bursting with mounds of silk. Marti felt that the setting sun looked like a woman with multicolored crinoline melting into the ground.

Alfredo greeted trees in Bear Mountain Park as though they were old acquaintances. Marti and Alfredo were gleeful hearing the grumbling of thunder as the skies shriveled into darkness over fields of gently waving grasses.

Juan volunteered to drive. They stopped at the Red Apple Restaurant on Route 17. Its rooftop plastic apple beckoned to them like a lighthouse. Everyone ordered hot dogs, hamburgers, or French fries. Their personal favorite condiment choices varied: sauerkraut, mustard, onions, relish, or ketchup.

As they ate, Evangelista prattled an endless stream of family gossip. "You heard that Tony is seeing Marti's friend Beatrice?"

"Uh, yes, we know...."

"What's the matter with her?" Evangelista asked.

"Why does she care?" Alfredo whispered.

Evangelista dispensed between little bites of French fries her own bits of gossip.

"She gets headaches and is so nervous."

"Yes-- and Tony likes her a lot. That's the main thing, right?"

"Oh come on, Alfredo. She's in her late twenties and never has been married. That is unusual for a Puerto Rican, "Evangelista joined in, looking around for any kind of kind of support.

Alfredo added, "Beatrice was the only child to stay with her mother for years after her father died. She finished high school at night here."

"Do you think he should date one of the Polish girls in Alfredo's factory?" Marti said.

Their conversation flowed like a downward stream. To veer from the sarcastic conversation, Evangelista related how strict their father had been.

"One night in Tampa, when Alfredo was sixteen, he wanted to sneak into town while our father was gone. But there was no gas in the truck."

Everyone gave Evangelista their full attention. "So Alfredo jogged over to our neighbor's farm and began siphoning gas from his truck. All of a sudden, gunshots rang out, and he felt a stinging in his back. He ran home, did not say anything. But my mother, she who saw everything - even though she wasn't there, made him take off his shirt. She found tiny birdshot wounds scattered on my brother's back, and several stuck in his side."

Evangelista stared sheepishly at her brother. He returned her side-glance with an irritable bite of his cheeseburger, packed with pickles and silver lettuce spilling onto his hand.

"I was lucky that time. Mother and our neighbor never said a word to Papa, dry-mouthed Alfredo said," Sis, remember 1931, when four of my friends decided to drive to New York from Tampa for an adventure? We had to sit in the open-air seat in the back of the car and got very burnt."

"*Sí*, you turned a red color, and remember when you got that job—after deciding to stay with Juan and me—pushing racks of clothes on Thirty-Eighth Street? You were always tanned."

"Sure enough, and my feet hurt."

Marti remembered. "That's the first time I saw you soaking your feet."

"It's good we left Tampa. I remember how the school officials tried to separate us, Evangelista, because of our different shades." All became quiet until Juan chuckled ironically and said, "Many peoples contribute to the great advances in any nation. The Romans built water systems in Spain. Then the Arabs continued improving the system with their inventions of cisterns and water wheels."

"Yes, but so many people are narrow-minded," added Anna remembering Lola's Long Island incident. She violently twisted her paper plate and tossed it into the garbage pail. They piled into the shiny reliable Chevy.

"Juan, I think we should turn right and continue up 17 to Newburgh."

"I don't know, Jimmy. Why don't we take 9W? The ride is much shorter," offered Anna from the back seat.

"No, Anna. It will take a while to get to 9W from here."

"It didn't last week, Juan, and besides, the views are better on 9W. First class!"

Anna and Juan began to argue in rapid-fire Spanish about the best route to take. The others tried to hush her. Jimmy twisted himself around and angrily said, "Well, Anna, you have your wish!" He turned the car around on Route 17 and headed back to the City. This gambit quieted down everyone.

"You can go back upstate. *Lo siento*. I'm sorry, but the stupidity of people should not spoil our day." Anna was too stubborn to admit that she had something to do with the tension in the car. They understood.

Alfredo broke the silence "You know what Mae West said?"

"No," replied Marti.

"A dame that knows the ropes isn't likely to get tied up."

A respectable belly laugh.

"A hard man is good to find," added a flushed -face Alfredo.

The joyous rollicking banter rippled on.

Anna spotted the sign "Villa Galicia—ten miles.

"This is near where Shorty opened his business."

"Who the hell is Shorty?" Evangelista piped up from the front seat.

"Carmen's son from the Club Regeneracion. The club provided a loan for him to open a business in a resort area in the Hudson Valley, north of Newburgh," Anna explained. She thought better not to mention her own loan to Shorty. Evangelista always wanted to know her business, although Anna also did her share of indelicate prying.

After their visit to Villa Galicia, the owner directed them to Sunny Acres. Alfredo, peering intently into the dance hall's window, "Did you see how much land surrounds this hall?" The wooden structure sat on a cement slab over a crawl space and had wide- screened windows. The two doors opened to a bar on the right, and an oblong forty-five foot room with tables and chairs off to the sides. There was a raised area for the bands. "Twenty acres, enough for the guests to take long walks in the woods when they're not dancing or drinking! And room to raise animals for slaughter," Marti said, recalling how her grandfather would ring the necks of chickens.

"Look! You see, guests are eating *pernil* and *pollo asado* in there. There's a kitchen in back. Imagine having the club bustling at two in the afternoon with the doors and windows wide opened, so you can spot the surrounding trees like in Cuban dance halls."

Anna replied, "Forty or more buses are rented each weekend for villa excursions. Shorty, the owner, told me that they run out of rooms for the guests who want to stay overnight." Marti slapped a bug that was maybe crawling on her leg.

"You got it! Yes, Anna, and we could put people up in our house when rooms here fill," said Alfredo dreaming of owning a resort himself some day.

"Okay, okay. How much would a small farm cost up here?"

"I think about eight thousand. We have two now."

The "villas" started to pop up in Plattekill after people from Spain's Castille Province settled in the 1920s and '30s, followed by Puerto Ricans. Farms were restructured into rooming houses. Meringues and pasa dobles were replaced by mambos. Velvet matador paintings hung over the dance floors at Casablanca, Sunny Acres, and El Nilo. The barns were reconstructed or rectangular buildings were built with shallow basements for supplies and with screens to allow cross breezes on hot summer nights. A bar and kitchen were located on one end and a band platform on the other, large enough to hold twenty or more musicians and singers who had come upstate ninety miles from New York City, bringing along the music of Johnny Pacheco, Celia Cruz, and Tito Puente. Crowds had prompted the owners to hire their own security to avoid confrontation with local police (who did not understand the language or culture)--- in case a recurring need to fight broke out between enemies. On one occasion, as a gaggle of preteen girls walked along the road near El Nilo Villa. One of them was accidentally struck and killed by a local man. State troopers, local police, and hired security had to hold the crowd back from attacking the driver.

Villa evenings were spectacles of rhinestones, tight sparkling dresses, and high heels on women of all hues, shapes, and ages. The children played outside, the little girls chasing fireflies and soiling their party dresses. The men wore suits with wide paisley ties and shiny mono or two-tone leather shoes. They sported fedoras at acute angles to bring out the fine shapes of their faces. Some donned dress slacks and button-down shirts, exposing their chest hairs and gold chains. Others wore plain polyester trousers with fine silk shirts.

Men at each table ordered a setup: glasses, ice buckets, and bottles of coke, rum, and whiskey to be shared among families and friends. Others sat or stood around the bar. Locals began to come to the villas—the exotic culture and sexy women intrigued the ones who liked the music. Some married into the Latino population, praying for something different in their lives. Alfredo's divorced sister, Ofelia, later married a tall, bow-legged farmer from the area.

Newburgh, the closest town to Plattekill, had in order of usage: churches, stores, insurance offices, a movie theater, and library.

Less than ten thousand people resided in the area. During winter, the villa owners worked in the service industries, including hospitals, schools, a military base; as well as in garment, pocketbook, and other factories. The children of the villa owners fought battles in their schools where they'd be called "spics" and "niggers" by children who only knew their own culture and history. It was taught that Columbus had discovered the Caribbean, while Indian artifacts were set on top of bookcases as though they were mere decorations without a history. Local family histories and heroes were emphasized in school. This was another handicap the new arrivals experienced, though some were taught cultural and family histories at home.

The lighter - skinned "Spanish" blended into the old population more readily than those with darker complexions. Their darker cousins, uncles, and friends challenged the biases of some in the white population. Some whites and African Americans did not respect cultures different from their own, while others accepted the diversity among Puerto Ricans as the wave of the future for this country--- despite its history of rabid prejudices and social ignorance.

Marti became pregnant again after Maria entered elementary school. But that did not alter their plans to move to the country. When Alfredo Jr. was born, his father could not wait to teach him how to milk cows, hunt, and fish. Alfredo and Marti were happy now that they had stopped considering an abortion. Two years before, when they had an unplanned pregnancy, they decided on an abortion. This procedure was illegal in the eyes of both the law and the church.

"Marti, it's up to you. I know how you were raised in the convent and all." She knew it was her decision, and probed at great length with Yesinia and Lola about it. She was surprised to learn that both went through abortions, Lola before she married; and Yesinia after the birth of their second child. Marti wanted to continue working and thought it would be stressful to have a second child before Alfredo's health stabilized.

Lola suggested a Cuban *curandera* who was well known in the East 110th Street area. Marti visited her several times for short chats. The *curandera* wanted to be sure that Marti thought this was the best solution for her and explained how a sterile instrument would be inserted to begin the process. When the cramps came, she would have to go to the hospital and deny knowing she was pregnant. Lola-- the only one who knew of her decision--accompanied Marti for the procedure. It resulted in cramps one day later and also in excessive bleeding. Alfredo rushed Marti to the nearest Catholic hospital. Together, they lied to the staff, particularly stressful for

Alfredo, who blamed his illness on Marti's decision. Only months later would Marti tell him what her hospital visit had really been like.

18 CAN YOU DO THIS?
1938

Marti knocked on Anna's door, instead of calling out her usual. "Anna, Jimmy, anyone home?!?"

Anna put down her newspaper, hoping Marti was not going to tell her Alfredo was ill again. He had been hospitalized five times in the years they had been married. He also had spent several weeks in Key West, visiting friends during the winter until his legs stopped swelling.

Heating the coffee left from breakfast, Anna asked Marti about her daughter.

"She's with her father in the park taking a break from her piano practice."

"Yes, Maria has a talent for playing. We were very impressed at her student recital, both how she conducted herself, and in her playing," said Anna.

Maria had diligently practiced for her piano recital. Now with long hair trailing down her back, she stepped onto the stage, sat down on the piano bench and with the lights dimmed, started to search the audience. "Ma, Ma, I can't see!" she called out. The lights were turned on after a moment as she regained composure and quickly began to play.

Marti was glad that Alfredo and Maria were in the park as she wanted to talk in private to Anna. The two women sat across from one another at the kitchen table. Anna knew there was something bothering Marti. She respected her "niece," even though they disagreed at times. She kept family matters private and seldom asked for favors, a sign of pride.

Marti finally said. "Anna, we still want to move out of the City."

"How can you afford to move with such a sick husband?"

Marti, twirled her thumbs, a habit she picked up from Anna. "What difference will it make if we live out of the City?"

Anna leaned over the table. "But his job in the City has union protection, Marti, and now he is assistant manager of the dye area."

"He'll commute."

"What if you move so far away, Marti, that he has to stop his work in the City?"

"We already talked about that. Alfredo could stay with his sister Ofelia and her husband during the week. Anyway, he could find a job in a nearby city with his skills."

"But who would hire such a man who takes off a month here and there?"

"We'll run a business in our house, a summer rooming house, like you and Jimmy do. After a while, he won't need to work outside the home," Marti insisted.

"It is not that easy---" said Jimmy, entering the dining room. "The mortgage, the taxes."

"The taxes will be less outside the City. We could raise some animals and sell the meat," Marti's head began to ache, her eyes darting between Jimmy and Anna.

"Does Alfredo know anything about rising animals?"

"Sure, Anna, they had cows and some chickens on their farm in Tampa."

"You mean you would milk cows and sell the milk?"

"Maybe, Jimmy, or sell the chickens and eggs."

"Well, there is a need for fresh eggs in the City," Anna acknowledged.

For an hour, she asked questions while Jimmy listened, as usual. He finally spoke:

"Oh?!? Marti can't even drive!"

"I'll stay home and care for the business." Marti tried to make it sound easy. But seeing the rigid expression on Anna's face made her own body tense.

"I want to make my own decisions without you always telling me what to do." Marti felt the tears almost exploding from her eyes.

"I'm tired of living in your home, tired of being treated as a child, tired of what goes on here." She shot an unsettling glance at glacier-faced Anna.

Anna lashed back. "What goes on here? You answer *me*! What goes on here you do not like?"

When Alfredo returned to their apartment Marti was feeding Maria. After some silence, he said that she looked upset.

"Anna always tells me what to do. I need her to listen to *me*! We will move whether she thinks it's a good idea or not!"

"Well, what did Jimmy say?"

"Not much. He did agree that the country would be better for the children."

Alfredo had asked Jimmy what he thought of them moving. If they could find a place they could afford outside of the City.

The next day at the dye factory on a cigarette break, the smoke drifted like clouds into the sun's rays, shimmering through the slanted windows held open by hanging chains.

"I think it's something you both want. So, therefore, you should try. You know that we worry about your health, Anna especially, but I see how much she likes the country. We talked about investing in property. We will help, of course, but maybe you could share your idea with others in the family."

An approaching co-worker interrupted. "Jimmy, what's the percentage of chemicals we should put in half a load of silk pillow cases?"

"Okay, start stirring the fabric… I'll be right there."

"Jimmy, the doctors say they cannot operate. A heart valve was damaged from an infection. Medication will slow the disease and make my heart pump stronger. I could stay home and just rest my heart. But y'know, that's not how I want to live… like an invalid. I'd rather die sooner and keep on living a full life."

"What about smoking?" Jimmy knew all about Alfredo's coughing.

"Yes, the doctor did tell me to stop. He claims my heart has to beat harder when I smoke," Alfredo took a quick puff on his cigarette before squashing it out.

"What kind of animals do you want to raise?" Jimmy asked him during lunch. He listened without saying a word. Then his winning smile flashed again.

"We mainly raised children." For good measure Alfredo added "Also, milking cows on the Tampa farm. But if we buy a small farm here maybe chickens and pigs. I liked that area with the villas. My brother, Tony, wants to move eventually. They both would like to spend time away from the City. His wife doesn't work now and knows how to drive. When business gets better, I will stay up there, or maybe find a part-time job. There are garment factories in Newburgh." Jimmy listened intently without saying a word. Alfredo's quick-pick solutions would later become complicated. But now his flighty dreams seem to push aside future obstacles.

Jimmy inched closer to him. "With this Depression, people are not traveling far for vacations or on weekends. Many enjoy the ride upstate like we do, and could eat lunch at your place. And their children could run around the farm. You know that's lots of people from Club Regeneracion would like a place to stay out of the City during the weekends. It's a good idea to share the place with others for the first year or until business picks up."

"You got it! The local newspaper in the area said that tourists are sleeping on lawns. We could provide a place to stay."

Several hours later in their bedroom, Alfredo broached the subject again.

"Why do you speak that way to Anna?"

"Anna is bossy. She even criticizes me for the way I discipline the children."

Alfredo knew the story. Maria had once changed a grade on her third-grade report card because she knew it wouldn't meet her mother's high standards. When Marti discovered the truth, she visited the school, walked into the classroom, and asked the teacher to step outside. Then she stunned the teacher by walking back into the classroom with Maria, pulling down Maria's pants in front of her classmates, and spanking her. Maria would carry her whole life the scaring from that incident.

Anna had told Marti that spanking was unnecessary punishment. Marti ignored Anna and her own deep-rooted anger. Inside her, there was a need to control, to mold at any extreme her children's behavior because she was convinced she was right.

"Why don't you leave Maria with Anna and go out and enjoy yourself more? I can't help seeing how nervous you are."

"Alfredo, I have something to tell you."

"What?"

"I'm pregnant again."

"You can't be! You're been breastfeeding, no? I thought you could not get pregnant."

"Me, too. But do you remember I suggested you begin to use rubbers again?"

"What will we do? Another abortion?"

"No! I can't go through that again! It was so painful when the woman started me bleeding. Oh, that nun at the hospital! *You sinned, did you not? You sinned by ripping God's gift from your womb.* Remember, Alfredo, the doctor stopped the bleeding with that instrument which burned me without any pain medicine? I spent a week in the hospital. They kept on saying that I had committed a sin and God will know what I did. It was horrible. You know they don't stop pregnancies at the Lady of Mercy Hospital."

"Oh, yeah! Lady of Mercy, my ass! We could take some of our savings and go to a private doctor who does scrapings early."

"No way, Alfredo. It's so expensive and if something should go wrong... Well, it's back to the hospital again."

"The hell with that hospital! You could go to another one, like Woman's Hospital."

"Yes, I could..." Marti supposed, her real feelings brushing away a tear.

Alfredo was silent. He felt guilty that his heart condition had something to do with her having an abortion.

"When my heart gets stronger taking the medicine, we'll have another," he tried to assure her. (But years passed after they agreed to stop birth control, and it took a while for Junior to be conceived. Alfredo Jr. was only four –months- old now and Marti, despite her breastfeeding, was pregnant again.)

"Don't cry..." Alfredo held her close. "You could ask Anna to help take care of Junior, and then rest after the baby is born."

"Yes, Anna does have experience caring for children and has a lot to offer us with her worldly background. It is difficult to rest with a newborn."

"There is enough space in this house to keep you separated. We could stay in our apartment, only going there to pick up the children. Maybe I can find daycare for Junior for a few hours until Anna completes her workday."

"Maria will suffer also. I notice how jealous she gets when we pay too much attention to Junior."

"Yes, Marti, I did notice that. Maybe it would be better if we asked Anna and Jimmy to watch Maria after school for us, and she can sleep upstairs some nights. I could drop her off at school in the mornings. I still think we need daycare for him so you could care for the baby and get some rest when the baby naps like you do now. I will also help with the feedings at night ... and on the weekends, of course."

Marti would ignore the stirring of her unborn during the day so busy was she with Alfredo Jr. But at night, she would sing softly for the baby in her belly to fall asleep. After a Sunday service, Marti confided to Father Pedro about her stress over the upcoming birth.

"My aunt, uncle, and husband work. They can fix it up between 'em to take and pick up Maria from school. I don't know who would watch Alfredo while I'm in the hospital."

Asking Evangelista was out of the question as she now had three daughters to care for. Besides, Marti was annoyed about that Polish co-worker being thrown at Alfredo before their marriage. Anna suggested she take time off from work. Marti felt the lingering anger pangs building up like the slow damming of a lake. *Is she blocking me again?*

"There's a home for orphaned children run by Sisters that I could check out for that week," earnestly replied Father Pedro. Alfredo was leery, but Marti recalled how caring the nuns in Cuba were.

The labor pains came suddenly and violently while Marti was feeding Alfredo Jr. Luckily, Alfredo was home and called a cab. The children were taken to Anna and Jimmy's home with strict instructions of where the baby would stay while Marti was hospitalized. The cab ride to Woman's Hospital on West 114th Street was quick, though the driver kept warning them that they'd have to pay to clean the backseat if Marti gave birth then and there. At that, Alfredo taunted him with comments like, "Oh ... the water broke all over the back seat. I'm so sorry. Marti, stop smearing blood on the window!"

The driver sped up, daring not to look at the mess.

Unlike the eleven hours Marti was in labor with Alfredo Jr., this delivery was to be quick. When they arrived at the hospital, the driver jumped out to inspect the back of his car. Alfredo burst out with, "I was only kidding. How much for the ride?"

The relieved driver told them to forget it and sped away as Marti was wheeled inside. The nurse glanced down as Marti's legs shot out, and she slumped down in pain, almost parallel in the wheelchair. The nurse spotted the bulged perineum.

"Mother, sit up! Cross your legs, the baby is coming!" Norma came out following several agonizing contractions after the efficient nurse slid off Marti's underpants. She positioned Marti onto the delivery table. She was still in street clothes.

"It's a girl, mother," the nurse sang out as she held the infant's feet and turned the baby upside down while the doctor rushed in to deliver the afterbirth.

Outside, Alfredo teared up as he was handed his second daughter, covered in a cheesy substance and bawling violently. "She looks like a ghost," he said in half-jest.

"Here is your papoose!" was the nurse's only response.

Norma was their third and last child. Lola and Alfredo helped as best they could. Marti looked tired most of the time. Alfredo picked up his son on Saturday in the orphanage on Twenty-third Street. While the building did look attended, he was shocked to see his son now. He found him in a diaper filled with feces, standing up holding the side of the crib and crying in agony from an ugly rash on his buttocks.

"Sister, what happened here?!?" he demanded.

"What is it?" The nun seemed unhelpful.

"What *is* it? What *is* it?" Alfredo threw the soiled diaper down to the floor. "I'm takin' my son outta here! How can you let this happen?" Alfredo continued cleaning his wrenched -in –pain son.

"Mr. Galindez, I'll call my superior," said the nun, rushing to the door as Alfredo dressed the baby. When the supervising Sister arrived Alfredo told her how he found his son.

"Well, we do our best here with the orphans," she countered in a dull, leaden tone.

"My son is not an orphan! Listen! Father Pedro assured my wife that he would be taken care of!"

There were no words from the supervisor to calm down Alfredo. "I will never set foot in another Catholic church!" he shouted, as he stormed out with his son tucked well inside his coat. And Alfredo stayed true to his word. He and Marti had such a heated argument that evening that the neighbors actually opened their windows and leaned outside to hear the harsh words. Anna and Jimmy never asked about it. They knew.

19 THE QUIET ZONE
1939

When Evangelista and her husband made the rounds to chat with family, each child would be given fifty cents and some time later, a dollar. All the children appreciated her kindness. She became the glue which held the family together as they struggled to raise their children. Evangelista sent homemade cheese to her family in Tampa. They'd sit around, eyes fixed on the cheese before eating it, admiring its physical appearance and discussing how it was made. She sent packages to her two brothers who had enlisted in the Army, and sent home V-letters. Ramon was the first to enlist.

Dear Marti,

How are you? I hope fine. I'm waiting to hear whether it's a boy or girl. I haven't written you in such a long time, but it's not my fault. It's really so hard to find something to write about over here. I haven't a thing to say except that I am well, but not happy being so far from home. I am doing nothing but sweating out my time in Ireland. It is a little better than being in England, but I'm stationed very far from the town, and there's nothing to do on the base to pass the time. I had a nice trip coming up here. It was a lot of fun, but it's very cold most of the time, and there's no place worth a damn to sleep. Well, I enjoyed it until someone borrowed my two blankets, and I almost froze to death that night. One thing here, the sun shines once in a while. It's not like England. It took a week one time before I saw the sun shine in England.

Well, how's the rest of the family? Alfredo still has a broken arm and can't write? Let me know! How is Maria getting along with the new brat, Alfredo Jr.? How does she feel about the little child that is on the way or is it here already?

Give my love to all.

Love,

Ramon

Alfredo had been helping his other brother lug wood up a ladder to repair windows in the building that Juan supervised and he fell, breaking his arm. Tony drove him to the emergency room of the local hospital. The doctor was amazed to hear Alfredo's heart with its bubbling, clicking sounds as the blood regurgitated around the defective valve.

"When I saw that---contorted--- look on his face, I told the doctor that I knew my heart was broken. But it was my arm that needed fixing," Alfredo joked.

Ramon was to return stateside and father four children. He started his own trucking business and, ignoring his chest pain, died at age fifty-five while repairing his car in front of his house. Nick enlisted right after Ramon.

Dear Marti & Alfredo,

Sorry not to answer your letter sooner, but they have been keeping me busy driving all through the South in search of jeeps, sedans, or command cars. You see, there's a division of Airborne troops that are having maneuvers and we're taking part. Our brigade has got the job of rounding up the equipment for the umpire and observers.

I don't know for sure, but maybe that will be my job all through the maneuvers, driving the umpires or correspondents around. I hope so. It will be a nice racket for about fifteen days. There's a lot of brass floating around here, even though the maneuvers don't start until the first.

I guess that's about all the news for now. How's everything with you all? How's Maria and Jr., plus the one to be? No wonder Jr. is getting heavy to lug around. After all, you're carrying two at a time! About the space for two young children and company, why don't you take a tip from the army and get a double-decker or a bunk?

Perhaps I'll be in the States a long time. You can't even volunteer anymore. The only way I'll make it overseas is if my whole outfit pushes out. Until then, I'm stuck here, and if my physical reports come in, who knows where I'll be?

Well, time to go. Regards to everyone and love to the family, until we meet again.

I'll remain, as always, yours,

Nick

Nick's outfit was sent overseas eventually, to somewhere in Sicily.

Hi folks,

How's the family? Fine and dandy, I hope. How's the new baby coming along? I am sorry to say that I don't remember its name at the moment.

By this time, you know where I'm located, so I'm afraid there isn't much to say. I can't write about the trip except to say that it got pretty interesting the last few days.

Took a recent trip in Italy, and we also passed through Paris. It was a very nice country.

Like I said, I haven't much to say, or much that I can say. I will start receiving mail soon from home. Oh, by the way, if you are going to send a package, please send cigarettes. They are like gold here, and just as valuable. Time to close. Give my regards to everyone, and love to the family.

As always,

Nick

"Why is Nick so vague about his work?" Marti prodded Alfredo in their apartment. It was June, 1939.

"He's involved in secret Army projects." Like a spy himself, Alfredo lowered his voice. "You know, like he's masterminding the invasion of certain German areas like … like Staten Island!

From somewhere in France, Nick wrote:

Hi folks,

Just a few lines to say hello. Everything is fine over here. I am as well as can be expected being so far away from everyone and all, but otherwise I am okay. I just received both your package and the V-mail letter, and that cough medicine really worked swell. As for the rest of the contents, the torrone really hit the spot. Only it makes me homesick. Reminds me of Xmas. As far as the "can," I'm savin' it till I need it. I am taking that "medicine" by the teaspoons so that it'll last me and a couple of my buddies. It really tastes good. It's been so long that I've drank any good stuff that it's almost unbelievable that kind of tonic still exists. It's a welcomed change from cognac and schnapps, which is slow poison, and even that you can't get here. The last time I had cognac was when I went on sick call with frostbitten feet, and the medic happened to have a bottle there for medicinal purposes, and that was up in the lines.

Well, enough about that. I was glad to hear that the children are all in good health. Jr. must be quite a big guy now. He's almost two, isn't he? Boy, when I get back, I am going to have to take a rehabilitation course just to know my family, including my own son. Only I hope he's not going to school by the time I meet up with him. If only these Krauts would wise up and yell, "Enough!"

Well, time to start closing. I have a few letters to finish tonight. Give my regards to everyone and all my love to the family.

As ever,

Nick

P.S. Pretty ironic about Tony, wasn't it? How's he taking it? A.W.O.L. (A Wolf On The Loose) now that he is divorced.

So long,

N

P.S. again, enclosing a picture I took in Nice. Been toting it around ever since. I'll try to have some more taken soon.

N

"Nick is surprised over Tony's divorce since he had sworn he'd never leave her despite their difficulties." Alfredo handed the letter to Marti.

"But that was over a year ago. Nick still doesn't know he is marrying Beatrice?"

"No, he's been gone for over a year."

A few years later, Nick was in the midst of battle in which he covered his men with continuous fire, even while surrounded by armed and firing German troops. He was awarded the Purple Heart. The left-leaning members of the family, many years later, would criticize him for training Green Berets during the war between rebels and the government forces in Latin America and elsewhere.

"God, I wish I could be there," sighed Alfredo after he finished reading the letter.

"...in Europe?"

"Exactly, Marti."

"If these Nazi threats increase---and if we go to war--- there are many things you could do right here like buy bonds, Alfredo." Marti was secretly glad, since the children were so young, that Alfredo's health prevented him from enlisting. And what of *their* dreams?

20 FULFILLED DREAMS
1940

The farmhouse was located across the Hudson River past the Red Apple Restaurant and Newburgh. Painted a mustard and mayonnaise yellow, the bi-level house sat along a gradual hill on Quaker Street. There were shuttered windows. Two barns, off to the side, couldn't be seen from the road. One had hay peeking out of the second story, and the other could hold cows or horses. Alfredo smelled cow dung from the farm down the road. There were fields on either side of the house. Across the street, the cleared land thickened with woods.

"Good hunting," Alfredo said to himself.

"This is so isolated," said Marti out loud.

The smaller barn was a good size for chickens. A fence made of narrow wood planks surrounded both barns. A windmill drew water by a rotating disk from a covered well. They didn't see the "For Sale" sign until they drove by it. They doubled back. Cats dashed from their view while barks from a hound filled the air as they climbed out of the car. As they approached the sign a the short-haired dog's ears shot up. Hoping they'd scratch his back it scampered up to them, tail swinging.

The farmer who answered the door peered curiously at the young Mediterranean-looking man with a thin mustache and a pretty woman by his side.

"Hello, I'm Alfredo Galindez. I noticed the 'For Sale sign and..."

"Come in, come in, friends," the old Quaker with the clean-shaved face, topped by a wide-brimmed straw hat said, pushing back the second dog, a collie that sniffed the hem of Alfredo's pants. "I will be pleased to show ye around. This here is the living room." The rectangular wide room had low ceilings, many windows, and was furnished with tired but comfortable furniture.

"This here is the dining room and through that door is the kitchen."

Marti loved the kitchen at first sight. It was partially submerged in the hill so the back wall had high narrow windows. The other sides of the house had many regular-sized windows covered with lace curtains that gently blew in the whistling wind. The sunlight glimmered through the curtain's lattice design and sprinkled the wooden floor with lively patterns. A single wooden table was complemented by ten regal Shaker-style chairs. Fire from the coal-burning stove could be spotted through the closed metal door with a handle that curved like a snail. The old refrigerator was made of black-and-white metal. The wrought iron stove had removable metal thick iron plates.

"That over there is coal-powered and will heat the whole house. My missus used to cook right on that flat part, but we got a range there," said the farmer, pointing. "That there stove is gas-powered. The Abbott and Mills Fuel Company are purty close by."

He scrambled up the wide stairs to show them the five bedrooms along the hallway. "Careful with these two steps," he cautioned. The rooms followed the slope of the hill, with a bathroom at the end of the hall.

"Ye folks live 'round here?"

"We live in the City, but I spent my childhood on a farm in Tampa."

"Oh, what type of a farm, Al?"

"Uh, call me Alfredo if... ye don't mind...We raised children mainly, but had milking cows also."

"I know what ye mean. My missus and I raised five children here. They're all but grown. The missus died a couple years back, so I'm movin' into one of my sons' farms in Clintondale. You folks know Clintondale?"

"Ain't that near Plattekill? We have friends who own one of the villas in Plattekill, the Perez family."

"You are Spanish then? A lot of those places are owned by Spanish people."

"We are Cubans--- or my wife is. My parents came from Cuba and moved to Tampa before I was born."

"Oh, so? I went to Cuba on our honeymoon. Something! We walked along that road by the sea in Havana, as the sun was setting. A real pretty sight it was."

"That was the *Malecón*," Marti clarified.

"That right? Well, we loved the way the pork was marinated with sour orange sauces and all that garlic. Yep, we had a real nice time: great shows at the hotel we stayed at. We visited Varadero."

"My school had vacations there. Did you visit the historical city of Trinidad?" asked Marti, looking into a closet. It was lined with pots, like polished surgical instruments ready for the next operation.

"No, we only had a week. Excuse me... Is that where cattle are raised?"

"Well, some. Also in Matanzas, a province to the east of Havana," Alfredo mentioned that his father had milked cows in Tampa, finding a comfortable connection with this American farmer.

"Well now, ye will do well to look at the barn out back."

They headed outside onto a dusty road and into a barn. Echoes of birds were filled in the air and tiny feathers floated near the ceiling.

Alfredo and the kindly farmer with the clean-shaven face turned the conversation to raising cows and then chickens.

"Ye could put the feed here. It's airtight." The farmer showed them a long wooden bin. "There is a coop. It's kinda of old but could be fixed out back. While scratch grain is the cheapest, I'd recommend the chicken feed mix at Sisti's. Yes, sir! Right on Main Street in Plattekill.... better quality. Cracked corn ye can fetch from Grimm's, down the road apiece." He led them over to two sagging bungalows. "This is good thing for company, but no heat, friend."

"For our summer guests," Marti whispered to Alfredo.

"Praise God, there are two coops over there rightly good for rabbits or chickens," said the farmer.

"How many acres you got here?"

"Oh, about a hundred and twenty-six, Al."

Alfredo winced.

"Good for grazing, parts of it are, and the rest is forest."

Alfredo shot a glance at Marti. His eyes told her that the farm was too amazing--and too expensive.

"How much you selling the house, barn, and bungalow for?"

He shrugged his shoulders. "Let's see, you're nice folks. How 'bout ten thousand? The land included. How's that, friends?!"

Alfredo sucked in his breath and said that they would have to talk to their family.

Back in the car, they agreed that even though it was too expensive, it was perfect for them. Particularly with the bungalows, even if they required work to rent out.

"For extra income, the coops in back are good for raising chickens and a few pigs," said Alfredo.

"Hey, why don't we ask Anna and Jimmy to help us? They made extra money selling that last brownstone, and they could come up on weekends." Marti's words surprised Alfredo. She knew they kept a financial distance from them.

"We'll need more than Anna and Jimmy could give us. Maybe I could ask my brothers if they'd be interested in using the place on weekends and for vacations."

"But what if someone wants out later because of money?"

"We could buy 'em out Marti, using money earned selling eggs or from the bungalow rental."

"I don't want anyone in my house, Alfred, no drifters."

"We are *all* drifters, going along this short narrow path until the end. And, well… Mine may be shorter than most."

"Alfredo, don't say that."

"Alright, my path will be long," he lied. "I'll continue working at the factory for a while." He glanced at Marti to sense her reaction, but already knew what she was going to say. So Alfredo continued, "Look, I could stay in the city during the week and come up on the weekends for a while when the weather is bad."

"What about your heart? What happens when you got to go to the hospital?"

"You know I get disability when I'm sick." Reading her face, Alfredo knew she was a whole lot skeptical.

"There are hospitals here, too."

"Well, hon, just haul my body to the nearest one."

Marti slapped him playfully on his slumped shoulder.

The Quaker farm owner, who told them where the Catholic Church was and agreed that it would be better to raise children away from the City, thought about Alfredo and the brother he later met. He decided the neighborhood needed a change from its usual people, particularly those Protestants. Some of them believed the Monroe Doctrine meant this country could meddle into those countries way down South. He didn't support World War I, either. Besides, the owner instantly liked the young man who shared his experiences raising cows for milking.

Marti and Alfredo approached Anna and Jimmy. They asked their opinion on the farm.

With the sound of radiator steam competing in the background "Jimmy asked, "Isn't the fifteen percent needed for a down payment and closing costs more than you have saved?"

"That is why we need partners."

"So how much down payment would you need, Alfredo?"

"About one thousand. Plus, we have two thousand in the bank. My brother will lend us one thousand. We need the thousand so we can get a mortgage and bank loan for building another bungalow and repairs. My salary will cover paying back the bank."

"You plan to do work in the area?" Anna asked, looking sympathetically right at Marti. No need to upset her.

"No, in the City and go upstate on the weekends," Alfredo said.

"Marti will stay up there all alone?"

"I don't mind, and Alfredo's usually away during the slow season anyway. And, you know, home when he does not feel well." Marti's voice trailed off.

Anna could not keep quiet. "You mean when he is in the hospital or at Key West."

"We'll make money from renting bungalows and selling chicken eggs. The area has some villas and we spoke to the Perez family. They are able to live on what they make in the summer. They're are usually short of rental space as are many of the other villa owners."

"How much can you make from rentals?"

"Enough, Anna, to pay one- half of the taxes and our year's living expenses," replied Marti too quickly.

"Sounds a little risky to me."

"Okay, but you know how much we do not like the City. There's enough of my family to keep the bungalows filled!"

"Marti, listen, without knowing how to drive how will you live alone with the children?"

Marti thought she would show them all how resourceful she could be, she who left that convent to go directly into a strict home in New York City---and then into a marriage. She could do this. She could learn to drive! Anna learned to drive, why couldn't she?

"Okay, let's think about this further," Jimmy said calmly. They all knew the conversation was over.

Privately, it was a whole different matter.

"Anna, do you think Alfredo will be able to work at the dye factory all week and then go sixty-five miles at the end of the week and work that farm?"

"I don't know, Jimmy. I'll call Tony's wife. She provided good accounting advise for us when we told her about the farm. Maybe she is willing to stay up there with Marti. You know she is disabled with those headaches."

"Her headaches?" Jimmy thought about the quiet woman whom Marti had met in the social club.

"Those headaches make it difficult for her, but the quiet of the country might help."

Six months later, in the early spring of 1940, Alfredo and Marti closed on the farm with his brother Tony, his second wife Beatrice, and Jimmy co-signing. Beatrice, out of work with blinding migraines, volunteered to stay with Marti for as long as it took her to learn to drive, and also do the farm's bookkeeping. Alfredo painted a sign that was nailed to a post dug into the ground by the mailbox. It read: "Villa Hispana."

21 THE VILLA
1940

Evangelista, Juan, and their daughters followed Alfredo. Their farm was located near a bend of Route 32 in Plattekill, adjacent to a pond whose occupants included dragonflies, gnats, whirling skating beetles, jellylike frog pawns, minnows, and in the basement—a tattered shelter with tree limbs—beavers.

Evangelista, the firstborn, who became a mother when her mother, Gertrudis, was giving birth to her siblings, continued the matriarch role of the Galindez clan. With her keen sense of business, she rented rooms and opened a roadside stand on the property.

Evangelista's aged wooden shed was converted into a stand where passersby could purchase empanadas, banana or papaya batidos; or a Cuban sandwich, pressed so that the cheese melted into the ham and pork. She flourished in her traditional role as the gracious elder. Her hospitality was the ring which kept the keys together. Their farm became the meeting place for the family regulars, who would come up each weekend and pitch in to help prepare food for themselves and for those who came to the café'. Surrounded by Americans (her term), Evangelista eventually tore up the photos of her mestiza mother to become "La Americana," with house and property. Yet she maintained the Cuban culture at home as Juan, dignified and thoughtful, spent quiet hours watching the sunset, reading, or in the shed behind the house. He sculpted metal objects from materials found at his job as a tool and die maker in nearby Newburgh. He later made a silver weight for his grandson when he graduated from medical school. While their prodigy studied, the entire family provided small gifts of cash or long-sleeve shirts. This grandson would later drive a motorcycle

on his rounds when not on duty as a resident to care for the health of hippie acquaintances.

The family would come together in Evangelista's bright spotless kitchen that was the size of two living rooms. The room had an institutional feel with the two sentry-like refrigerators that sat on either side of the pantry door. The pantry was the size of a bathroom with a small window overlooking a back flagstone patio. The kitchen table, surrounded by twelve chairs, was covered by a plastic oilcloth. Guests would impulsively rub the shiny oilcloth as they engaged in conversation while Evangelista (who never again worked outside of her home) stretched dough over and over then rolled into pie crusts.

The kitchen led to a formal dining room with a mahogany table, covered by a lacey tablecloth, seldomly used as company assembled in the kitchen. The tablecloth matched the curtains hugging the thick window frames. Adjacent to the dining room, the front foyer opened its arms to the front door that lead onto a columned porch. Bordering the foyer was the living room (with a piano), the length of the dining room and kitchen. It would be played by a grandson who liked to hide in the barn to smoke pot. (For most of their sixty-year marriage, Juan and Evangelista shared the bedroom filled with cozy-looking wicker furniture located at the far end of the living room). The upstairs bedrooms were reserved for the children and guests. Her brother, Tony, whom she called, "my little brother," even when he was well into his fifties, built pens for the pigs that were fed table scraps as they grunted their approval.

They sat in Alfredo's kitchen by the coal-burning stove during a weekend visit. "Which type of chickens do you intend to buy, Alfredo?" Anna asked.

"Our neighbor on Quaker Street suggested 'silkies' because they hatch white eggs and are good-natured," he replied. "They have a dual purpose— provide meat and there's egg production."

"Why don't you ask the feed store what they think best for the local weather?"

"Really, Anna? I didn't know you were such an expert."

"I was just trying to use common sense. The chickens who lived in Tampa may not make it in the North."

"My neighbor raises chickens for his family and should know. His chickens do better than I do healthwise during winter," Alfredo answered with his usual biting charm.

Twenty-five boxed bird-talking chicks arrived.

"Are they all girls, Alfredo?" Anna pressed her nose briskly into a furry ball.

"I guess they *are* all girls. I asked the store to send me all girls."

"How can you tell if they are girls?"

"Just look between their legs and if there is no penis, it is a girl," he said evenly with a wry smile.

Marti picked up several chicks and looked between their legs.

"I don't see anything" Alfredo howled.

"No, really, check out their rear ends and squeeze out some excreta. If there's a bump inside it's a male, no bump a female. Didn't you notice the chickens your grandfather had?"

"Not really, they just ran around, and I washed the feathers and dirt off their eggs. So the eggs come from these cracks?" Marti held the chick upside down.

"Yes, that's where mature eggs come from. I can't tell, Marti, which are the females, but even a professional sexer at the hatcheries will only be about ninety percent right. So we may have a rooster or two. Still, we need 'em to help fertilize the eggs if we want more baby chicks."

The chicks were squeezed into a heated brooder for six weeks when their feathers replaced the fuzz the children had rubbed their cheeks against. Alfredo Jr. provided fresh water daily.

"Why do they poop in the water?" Marti innocently inquired.

" Because they are dumb," Alfredo dutifully replied.

"Dumb birds, here dumb birds," repeated Junior while chasing a few.

Marti opened the barn door and the chickens ran out, encircling them as she threw the corn stored in her apron pocket.

She strolled over to the coop where the chicks were kept under several bulbs and picked one up. She began to put one chick down, and then squeezed its midsection. No poop came out. She turned the bird upside down and squeezed again. A stream of gray poop shot out and hit her in the chest. She squeezed again and looked and saw no bump---a female! The chick began to emit shrill noises, morphing into a mass of quivering yellow feathers. She ran to the hose and washed off the toothpaste-like substance. She would not mention this to Alfredo so as to avoid the story becoming another one of his jokes.

"I want chickens for sopa de pollo."

"I'll call the hatchery and ask for a few old birds, but you have to promise me that you will help kill them."

"Why not?" It was a lie. No way would Marti hold a dying chicken flapping like newspaper during a storm.

"I'm only kidding. You just do the great cooking, and keep my bed warm." "I have my own big chick here, and that is enough," he said in a soft, loving tone, grabbing Marti by the waist and hugging her until she screamed, "I can't breathe."

"You know, Anna asks too many questions about the chickens."

Marti agreed. "Yes, but you know how to handle her."

"I'm glad we have the bungalow for family and all the land to keep her far from us. She will not hear you moaning and *gritando* at night."

"I don't scream, Alfredo."

"Yes, you do."

"No, I don't."

"I should tape you!" Alfredo lavished kisses on her mouth and neck.

He came home by Metro-North each Friday night or by car with Anna and Jimmy, who helped inject the chickens with immunizations. Alfredo Jr. would run to the car each of those Fridays, Alfredo immediately lifting him up into the air. As he held Norma on his lap, Marti filled him in on the week's activities.

Norma would grow as open and natural as the fields and the animals she played with. With her laughter and sunny outlook, she blossomed into an outgoing, free-spirited child. As soon as she could walk, she would tag along with Alfredo, chattering to him as farm chores were attended to.

Fond of all her animals, there was actually only one chore that horrified her: the slaughtering of hogs.

Jimmy and Tony held tightly onto the hog. Alfredo would quickly slice its throat with a carefully sharpened knife. The animal convulsed violently until shock set in from blood loss. It collapsed against their bloodied pants and rubber boots. Then it slid onto the ground.

After the body was hosed down another quick cut exposed the gray omentum, followed by other slices. The slippery, glistening intestines flopped into waiting pails followed by pieces of loin, fat, and shoulder. The dogs ogled the scene from a distance. Organs were removed and thrown to the dogs, whose mouths stained red as they chewed. The intestines were carried to the kitchen sink, washed in salted water, checked for leaks, and chilled so the casings could be stuffed and made into sausages.

The chilled loin, shoulder, and fat were sprinkled with vinegar and ground in a metal sausage grinder. The meat was flavored with spices, such as garlic, paprika, salt, coriander, cloves, and pepper. A funnel-like metal sausage-stuffer was fastened to a wooden table, filled and turned by a thick wooden handle. The piece of intestinal casing was secured over the spout of the sausage stuffer. The sausage mixture was fed into the metal chamber and the stretching casing was filled to a one-inch diameter sausage. Air bubbles were worked out. When the sausage was six-inches long, an extra inch of casing was pulled and twisted into a tie, followed by filling the next link. The sausages were refrigerated to mature the flavor and to make them firm.

The salted pig carcass was pierced by a sharpened six-foot pole, a handle screwed into one side, and suspended onto the V of two slingshot-shaped stumps that were drilled into the ground. The pit was filled with ignited charcoal. The pig was slowly turned and marinated with olive oil, garlic, and other flavorings for many hours. The skin turned a chestnut-rust color.

Marti would prepare trays of rice and chicken in the oven where each rice grain could be counted. The dish would then be served to the vacationing guests on their hacienda. "Alfredo, why are you late?" she asked one Sunday.

"I had to drive back to that country store because that American did not give me the right change."

"You mean at Sisti? Well, he's always fair with me. For sure"

"Okay, it was an oversight, but we must let these people know that we're as smart as they are. Probably smarter in my case." Huge smiles and hugs. "This is not a *Encomienda* situation."

"What's a *Encomienda?*"

"Well, I'll try to get it right. In the 1500s, Encomienda was Cuban land, native people lived there. But the land was owned by friends of the Spanish land administrators. Many natives---too many--- died from harsh living conditions.... diseases brought by the Spaniards. Many hundreds ran away to the mountains. Like we have, you know, before the city diseases caught up with us," he suddenly broke into laughter.

"Okay, now I remember some of that from school."

"*Si, Marti*, there were some native peoples who ran to silver-rich Mexico or committed suicide rather than work on stolen land. This is our land--thank God!" Alfredo said, his eyes turning misty.

22 THE GHOSTS REMAIN
1940 - 1941

The untouched forest was used only for hunting pheasant and deer. There were three acres maintained around the farmhouse, barn, and the two bungalows rented to guests. Alfredo's prediction was correct. Reservations had to be made in early spring to secure a bungalow. A room in the farmhouse remained vacant as reservations were overbooked in case someone canceled at the last minute.

"Alfredo, wake up! You said you wanted to feed the chickens," called up Marti from the bottom of the stairs. When he did not respond after she called twice, she went upstairs. She shook him. As he turned she noticed his pale, clammy skin.

"Alfredo! Oh my God, Alfredo!"

He barely whispered it, so short of breath.... "Call the doctor...call..."

Doctor Shapiro lived five miles away. He was forty-five, an oval-faced man of medium build, who always wore thin-framed glasses. His parents had worked in the garment industry on the Lower East Side of New York. Following his examination of Alfredo he quickly gave him an injection. He helped Alfredo to the bathroom, where he passed large quantities of urine.

When they returned to the bedroom, Marti was standing at the doorway, her stomach churning. Dr. Shapiro turned to Alfredo, "I will have to take the excess water from your knees." He exposed his patient's swollen legs. "Your heart is weak. It can't circulate your body fluids, and they're accumulating in your legs."

Marti could not bear seeing the pain on Alfredo's face and left the room.

Thirty minutes later the doctor came downstairs, where Marti was waiting anxiously for him to finish the procedure.

"Your husband is better. I stepped up his heart medications.

Here are samples you can use before you pick up more at Seaman's. He needs to take it easy. Is he still working in the City?"

"Yes, he came up last night on the train."

"Does he still smoke and eat salty foods?"

"Yes---both."

"He should stop! I know a man has to work, but the smoking has to stop. Do not put any salt on the table, and add only enough to taste in his food."

"Honestly, how is his heart, doctor?" Marti felt the churning in her stomach coming back.

"Mrs. Galindez, he is young, which is in his favor. The valve does not work well, so some of the blood flows back and then forward again. That makes the heart work harder than it should be working, and it's already quite enlarged."

Marti thought back to the times she had rested her head against Alfredo's chest and had hearing the irregular heart beats. "Doctor, should he stop working? I told him, I told him--"

"I spoke to him about that. For now, he will take off only a few weeks... if he still feels weak on Sunday. A man is got to do what he feels is important. But please tell him again to stop smoking and cook with as little salt as you possibly can."

Dear Marti,

Hope you and the children are well. I went fishing again today, a good time to think about things: smoking has to stop, and I will bring my lunch from home as you suggested.

Did you pay the mortgage on time?

Miss you all,

Alfredo

Marti could smell the sea on the paper.

Dear Papa,

I miss you very much. I wish you could be here. Did you catch any fish? Are you having fun?

I have dancing lessons in school now. I hope I get a good report card.

Love from your little monkey,

Maria

Dear Alfredo,

I am very glad to hear that you're feeling better.

Junior recently saw that snapshot of you in a boat and wants to know when you will take him boating.

This past Friday night I went to Leptondale School, where we played cards while Maria and Norma played games. I also went to the Morris Paint Shop. The man there asked for you and when I told him where you were he said that Morris was in Miami. He gave me his address to send to you. Maybe you could send him a card. You do remember the old man from the hardware store on Broadway? His address is:

Morris Rosenblum

Hotel Leslie

Ocean Drive 13th St.

Miami Beach 39, Florida, 33139

He said Morris would be glad to hear from you. I know you don't like to write but am sending the address anyway.

Evangelista and Juan left Saturday for Tampa on Saturday. They came to say goodbye the other day and to take the battery and little gift for Graciela. I felt like going with them.

The Monday after you left I got a card from Lola. They are also in Key West. If we would have gotten in touch before, you could have driven down with them.

Maria did well in her report card as usual.

As ever,

Love,

Marti

Alfredo read and reread the letters. He planned to visit Graciela during the week, and she would know where Lola and Carlos were vacationing. "These Cubans keep track of one another as if by mind-radar," he mused with a chuckle, remembering the time Lola and Carlos came to visit Villa Hispana. They shared jokes, drank, and played cards until 1:00 a.m. He had time now to think back over the good times with friends. This season, he and Marti would open their doors again, perhaps for the last time.

He knew that he was not getting better. The arduous farm work was becoming even more difficult. Unless he quit his City job he would not be able to take the pressure building up. He hid this from Marti, but her suspicions rose when he would return from the City on Fridays and go right to bed after dinner.

After waiting all week to be with her father, Norma's excitement peaked seeing him walk off the train. She would often search his pockets for the candy or gum he never neglected to bring her. She would then sit on his lap for the trip back to the farm. On the most recent Friday, however, Alfredo ignored Norma upon his return trip from the station. He took his shambling body directly to the bedroom. Disappointed Norma chased after him.

"Alfredo, Norma was talkin' to you when you walked out of the room!"

"O.K., give me a break, Marti. I didn't sleep well last night at my sister's apartment." Alfredo took off his shirt and set on his bed.

"You used that excuse last week, Alfredo. When I call your sister you're always out. What are you doin' in the City? Are you going out to dinner with that Polish girl maybe... or something?"

"You are crazy, Marti! You're too damn sensitive and never forget a slight. Lay off!"

"Excuse me! I work all week. I'm with your children day and night, and ...!"

"Why don't you recite the rosary for relief, Marti?"

"Don't you start that again! Just because you are a nonbeliever..."

"Marti, please, don't you remember what those nuns did to our son?"

"Okay, they did not take care of him, but they are only human... not God!"

"Did God tell the priests to brand and support the killing of all those in Latin America who wanted to keep their own religions?"

The bickering dragged on all weekend until on the Beacon train platform they apologized to each other on Sunday evening.

Maria heard the nagging back and forth from her room, her mixed-up thoughts racing. How could she make the situation better? Show her mother how she did like caring for the two brats. No! She partly blamed them for her parents' lack of attention toward her.

Alfredo realized Marti's stress over the children. Now she baked homemade bread with very little salt as the doctor suggested. During his next trip to Florida, he sat alone on the Key West dock, conjuring up ways they could save money if he had to quit his job. As a pelican flew overhead, Alfredo felt like leaving his own body and joining the flight of birds over the bay... No awareness of himself. None.

Alfredo had been gone this time for one month. Marti stayed on the farm with Tony's wife, Beatrice, who spent hours in her room suffering from her headaches. Seeing her talking to herself, Marti suspected that Beatrice, a very sweet, sensitive woman, suffered from a distortion of rational thinking. Still, she kept quiet about it.

"Marti, I think her mind does not work well," Anna had warned. "Should I take a leave at work and help with the children?"

"No, she helps, really," Marti didn't want Anna around with her busybody ways. Beatrice was easy to be with, and the children enjoyed her company. She shared Marti's religious beliefs.

"God will protect, if you do the right things. God will reward you, maybe not here, but in heaven for sure," Beatrice would say. She was a quiet, thoughtful woman with a serene smile who had no children of her own but loved to play with Marti's.

Beatrice had been warned by a doctor about the pills. If she took these to treat her headaches, they might harm her unborn. Tony knew that Beatrice would talk to herself at times. When he first noticed the odd behavior, he thought she was praying. He could no longer fool himself. This was his second marriage, though, so he planned to stick it out.

Beatrice worked for ten years as a bookkeeper in a store that sold auto parts near Long Island City until the company moved to New Jersey. Tony, whose hospital carpentry job was stable, agreed that Beatrice could help Marti as the farm bookkeeper until he retired and moved upstate. Tony had separated from his first wife, who remained in the Bronx with his son while Tony moved to Long Island. Some of his brothers had married "American" girls, but he preferred ones who smelled of coconut oil to Americans who used Vaseline, and could not dance the mambo. He would laughingly relate this to Alfredo, who shared his offbeat sense of humor. Tony had seen how ill Alfredo could become and thought it best that his wife stay close to Marti. Perhaps deep inside him he wished to maintain space from Beatrice and her strange whispering. Besides, Marti had the responsibilities of working and caring for the children while Alfredo was recuperating from one of his "spells."

"The eggs were selling well, Beatrice---both in the City and in the country." Marti smelled the familiar odor of feces mixed with feed as she and Beatrice picked the straw spotted eggs.

"Here's the water pail," Marti said. "Just rinse off some of the dirt. Folks don't mind a little hay. I'm going to wash the shit off these two chicks, so it doesn't harden."

Beatrice laughed and watched Marti run after the chicks. She still thought that moving to the farm was a great idea. She was getting fewer headaches, even though it meant that for a couple of months she would see Tony only on the weekends and holidays. She talked to the voice she heard ... but less now.

"You know, I saved the day when Junior came screaming from the field behind the shed! Marti and I ran to meet him, but could not come too close as he smelled so foul," confided Beatrice to her voice. She would soon be put on medication that would control the new voices.

"Junior, you smell like a skunk!" shouted Marti, falling onto her knees unable to move.

"A pussy cat, a pussy cat there!" Junior pointed to the skunk that was running into the woods.

Its fluffed-up tail stood straight, like a gigantic feather. Marti screamed so loud that Junior backed away.

"My God, did he bite you?"

"No, Mama. No, Mama!"

Marti stood up. "What do we do?"

"Come here, Junior!" Beatrice yelled, then ran to get the hose and dragged it toward him.

"Take off your pants, your shirt--- everything!"

"Mama...?" He choked on his tears.

"Yes, take off your clothes like Aunt Beatrice says."

She hosed him, the water nearly throwing the three-year-old off his feet.

Beatrice handed the hose to Marti and ran into the barn, returning with a shovel. "Take him inside and wash him good. Don't forget his hair!"

Beatrice quickly dug a hole next to the shed and picked up each garment with the shovel, throwing them into the hole. Then she covered the hole with dirt. She helped Marti search Junior's body for bite marks.

"What a stupid little jerk!" was Maria's curt reaction to the story that night.

After Maria left the kitchen Marti said, "I notice how jealous Maria gets if we pay too much attention to Junior."

"Yes, I noticed that, too. Maybe you could ask Anna and Jimmy to give her special attention when they visit," ventured Beatrice while bathing Norma. "I could drop her off at school in the mornings some days. Maybe you need daycare for Junior several afternoons a week. You can care for the baby and get some rest when the baby naps."

"Daycare around here? No, Beatrice, I see how you enjoy caring for Junior." Marti considered herself lucky to have Beatrice during the week when Alfredo was at his sister's house.

"I'll help with the feedings, of course," Alfredo volunteered that weekend. Sitting by the kitchen stove, he worried how Marti looked tired most of the time, and remembered her delusion that he might be playing around in the City. Marti worried that one of the children would wander off again. He agreed to help with the driving classes that Beatrice had bravely begun. Driving did not come easy for Marti. But it was a necessary skill in case of an emergency when Marti was all alone with the children. Alfredo would not admit to her his own exhaustion, which made the weekend farm chores unbearable lately. They had wished for this farm for a long time, and he wanted this life to continue. But like a foggy dream, hope for a longer life was fading fast.

Marti remembered how angry she would be at the children before Beatrice came to live with her, particularly when Alfredo was in Key West.

"Norma, stop wiggling!" Marti yelled as she bathed her daughter in a metal pan set on the floor next to the stove. But she knew, of course, that Norma's fussing was typical for a toddler. It had been snowing for days. Marti had just finished shoveling a path to the mailbox so that Maria could catch the school bus. Beatrice was visiting her husband in the City, so could not travel upstate until the roads were cleared. Neighbors had not come to visit her as they usually did. So she was stuck in the house by herself with the children for five days.

"Norma, if you don't stay still, I will pow pow you, *malcriada!*"

One hour later, only Norma's lingering whimpers would wake Marti from her deep sleep. When Marti heard those sounds get louder, she ran into her daughter's room and picked her up, feeling her wrench under her. When she removed the diaper, Norma's buttocks were puffy and reddened.

"Oh, my God, I burned you against the coal stove!" She rushed to the cellar for a raw potato, cut it in half, and gently rubbed Norma's buttocks.

"*Lo siento, lo siento*, I am sorry" she cried out, noticing the child pulling away from her--- and turning onto her stomach to suck her pacifier.

Oh, God, help me with all this. Alfredo is right... I need rest.... She remembered how upset she became at other small incidents, like what happened in Newburgh.

"Marti, do you want a lift to town while I go to the dentist? You could do some shopping," a few days later asked her neighbor, who owned the dairy farm down the road.

In case she got home from school before they returned, Marti left a note for Maria. They drove the ten miles to Newburgh, after which Marti stopped by Texas Weiner for hot dogs, covered with onions in a thick brown sauce, as a treat for the children. Then they headed to the butcher shop.

"Hello, Mrs. Schwartz...", wiping the last of the brown sauce from Junior's mouth. "Give me three pounds of ground beef please, and two skirt steaks for ropa vieja."

"Big snowstorm. Glad you found someone to drive you into town while your husband is in Florida... How is he?"

"...better, coming home in March."

"Oh, by the way, do you know someone who could clean my house? We lost the girl who worked for us."

"Why don't you ask one of those women coming over from Poland? There are plenty Jewish refugees now!" Marti said, her face burning: *This lady thinks because I am not a white American I would clean her house. Me! I own my own business, too. Maybe she thinks I have a cleaning lady.* Then she laughed to herself, remembering that Alfredo always called her (in a funny way) too sensitive. She paid the woman, who remained silent. From the frozen-faced look on Marti she obviously understood that she had offended her.

23 THE SEPARATION
1941 - 1950

Flames licked the sky. Bombs shredded metal. The sea caught jumping men.

"Black smoke is blinding them!" screamed the radio announcer.

It was Sunday, December 7, 1941. Life slowed down as the movement of the tree branches were laden with snow. Paths were shoveled around the barn and to the mail. The tall field grasses poked their dried heads above the snow.

"Come in! We are being attacked!" Marti called out to Alfredo, who was in the yard feeding chickens.

"Are you drinking rum in there?" he shouted back.

"Alfredo, the Japanese just bombed us!"

"Well, they missed the house and barn," he teased, washing his hands in the kitchen sink.

"Now… who was bombed and where?"

"In Pearl Harbor, Hawaii."

The war surged. Now barges and dry docks were built in Newburgh to repair war-related vessels. Meat, sugar, gasoline, and coffee were rationed.

"We could kill a chicken or a pig for meat," Alfredo tried to assure Marti.

Later, they sat in the living room reading newspapers.

"Alfredo, while guys are going to war and working on ship repair, I could apply for the work they left in the States… but part-time." His pressed - together lips showing disapproval did not escape Marti.

"I think your job is caring for three children and our business. We're doing better. People are coming here for vacations because of the war."

"That's true," was Marti's answer. But the angry look on her sleep-deprived face did not match what she said.

"Please stay home, Marti. I know you get frustrated with the children, but please wait until they are older before you leave 'em."

"They're hiring at Stewart Air Force Base. Mr. Cumulada got a job in the cafeteria. Remember the tasty ropa vieja he prepared?" Marti was unable to hide her disappointment.

"Mira, Marti." Alfredo read Newburgh's selection for a study to put fluoride in the drinking water. Then he glanced at his wife in hope of changing the subject again. "Look at all those factories in Newburgh notebooks, pocketbooks, carpet-making, wool, silk, and cotton weaving. You can get a job dyeing locally!" she said. How gaunt Alfredo looked lately. She kept that to herself.

"I can't dye carpets or pocketbooks, Marti!"

"Evangelista thinks Juan is paid well as a tool- and- die maker on Lander Street."

"I would have to retrain to do what Juan does," Alfredo said louder.

"Stay with dyeing, but change where you work." Marti tried to sound calm, so Alfredo would not know how concerned she really was.

"Don't you see the problem with starting up in a new place? They may let me go if I have to take time off. Jimmy and Pasqual cover for me. Pasqual works part-time and appreciates the extra hours." Alfredo felt tired because Marti would not leave this subject alone. Sitting in his favorite chair gave him little comfort. Weekends lately were tense. He spent more time hunting or visiting the neighbor who owned a chicken farm on Union Avenue. Quiet time. He noticed how much Marti screamed at the children.

"Come over here, Marti, *mi amor*. Are you not happy here with all the chickens instead of the *bandidos* in the City?" He encircled her, lifted her up, and gave her a long kiss while waltzing her toward their bedroom, transforming the movement into a tango. She followed his twists and backbends. He let her go, performing a few rapid foot movements, reaching for her again as they approached the door.

"Mommy!" Norma called down from upstairs.

"I'll go. Where is her milk?" Alfredo, danced his way to the refrigerator.

Beatrice, a month later, proved to be invaluable once again. She suggested, based on the farm's financial records, that Alfredo could leave his job in the City and apply for temporary disability. If his heart condition improved, a return to part-time work would be a future consideration. He could concentrate on the farm whose profits had steadily increased. Alfredo reviewed the financial records and discussed the matter with Jimmy, who reassured Alfredo that the dyeing job would be waiting for him. Alfredo applied and was granted disability payments.

The routine of farm life and raising the children tempered the years. Alfredo felt physically stronger. Several years went by until grey days set in again.

"Not so deep Doc, please!" The needle was pulled out half an inch. The remaining inch was embedded laterally to the knee joint.

"Ouch!" Alfredo recoiled his torso as the needle searched for the fluid seeping from his blood vessel. His damaged heart valve skipped beats.

"I'm done," said Dr. Shapiro, quickly removing the needle and filling the container with two hundred cubic centimeters of rusty-colored fluid. "Have you been taking your pills, Mr. Galindez?"

Maria listened at the door. She felt a hand grab her collar. "Don't you ever go into the room when Dr. Shapiro is here!" Marti admonished her daughter.

"But he's hurting Daddy."

"I know, but it has to be done. Go on, now!"

Marti entered their bedroom, distressed to find Alfredo's knee bandaged, as if he had a soccer injury. Removal of fluid saved his taxed heart muscle. She hated that syringe of bloodied fluid. Droplets of blood spotted his sock.

"Good, Mrs. Galindez. I'm glad you're here. Alfredo's diet must be as low as possible in salt."

"I make low-salt bread."

"Good. What about his smoking? *Still* doing that, Mr. Galindez?" He turned to Alfredo, whose eyes pierced the doctor's.

"Well, it's better," Alfredo admitted.

The doctor knew from seeing Marti's eyes tighten fiercely that Alfredo smoked as much as before.

"Please, let's give that heart some rest. No smoking. None! Nada! It narrows the blood vessels. Your heart works harder."

"Yes, boss," Alfredo said, with a forced smile. Dr. Shapiro had grown close to the family, who paid him on time. And, despite his objections, provided a dozen fresh eggs each visit. He was concerned about Alfredo's thinness over the past year.

Spring came. It was time to begin preparing for their weekend guests. Alfredo had been right. There was plenty of work on the farm. Business was continuously picking up. Anna and Jimmy brought twenty dozen eggs to the city on Sunday evenings to sell to regular neighbor customers.

Within two years, however, Marti and Alfredo would have to make plans to sell the farm. They had paid the first installment on building a house located on a nearby main road. Because of Dr. Shapiro's dire warning. Tony and other members of the family began discussing ways the farm could stay in the family.

"Alfredo, if you want to see your children grown, you must stop working. The farm has become a physical burden to keep up." His family agreed, and Tony and Beatrice prepared to rent a house in the area.

Alfredo had spent two months not getting better, in Key West after his legs swelled up.

"I can come and tap the water from your knees every other day. Or you can go and rest your heart in warmer weather."

Marti felt her stomach churning again but did not make any suggestions. She knew how it was without Alfredo around to help her but also how dangerous the fluid accumulation was on his heart Maria was just beginning middle school and the younger children were in elementary school, so she could not join him. Besides, who would look after the farm?

Two days before Christmas. Marti woke when she heard Alfredo coughing in the bathroom. She found him sitting on the toilet, leaning on the sink, short of breath and sweat dripping down his face. She looked up, to see stark fear in his eyes.

"I'll bring your extra pajamas. Evangelista and Juan are on the way." The men carried him into the ambulance as Marti worried they would slip on the icy driveway.

"Don't forget to pay the mortgage, Marti," he managed to say gasping for breath.

"You will be back before the end of the month." This would be the second Christmas his heart took him away from her.

"I don't think I'll be comin' home this time." His eyes welled up.

"Don't say that. You always get better... Just rest. I'll take care of everything."

Anna, Jimmy, Marti, and the children exchanged gifts quietly the next morning. Marti had trouble finishing her breakfast, feeling the ache again in her stomach. She impatiently listened for Juan's car so he could take her go to the hospital. Evangelista stayed with the children. Marti spent the afternoon sitting in the lounge, waiting to visit Alfredo for the allotted ten minutes every hour that the ICU permitted.

Seeing saw him struggling to catch his breath, she held his hand.

"When will he be able to go to a regular room?" she quizzed Dr. Shapiro, who avoided her gaze.

"First, we have to stop his heart pumping so fast and irregularly, Mrs. Galindez." The doctor was amazed that Alfredo had avoided hospitalization for the past six months. His heart muscle was so enlarged from the strain of the damaged valve that it was a miracle he had not been back sooner. *"Such a young man, it's a shame,"* the doctor thought, at the same time trying to reassure Marti that it was just a matter of getting rest.

The phone rang the next day at 7:00 a.m. Maria picked it up, still in her pajamas.

"Mother, it's some man."

Marti thought it might be someone from the coal company checking when he could deliver.

"Mrs. Galindez, is that you?"

"Yes."

"It's Dr. Shapiro."

Marti sat on the floor.

"Mother ..." Maria said faintly.

"I have bad news. Are you alone?

"No, my parents, my children ... my children ..."

Your husband died this morning at 6:50. They did cardiac massage on him, but his heart did not respond, nor did it respond to medication ...I am so sorry Mrs. ..."

"I know..." Marti dropped the phone as tears started to flood her face.

"Mommy, what happened?" Maria said, picking up the phone. She could not speak. Marti handed the telephone to Anna running into the room. The doctor spoke gently to her. "Take your time coming in. We will hold the body until you arrive."

"When did he die?" she finally said.

"At 6:50 this morning."

"We will be there in twenty minutes, depending on the roads." Anna hung up the phone and sat down next to Marti, crying convulsively on Anna's shoulder.

"What happened?" Jimmy hearing the moans asked,. "He's not..."

"Yes... My Alfredo has left me all alone. I can't believe it. He said he was not going to make it this time. Only thirty-nine. My poor Alfredo, my poor Alfredo... my poor Cubanito, I wish I had stayed in the hospital. I could have been with him. I could have warned the nurses."

"No, his heart was bad for a long time," Jimmy hardly got the words out.

Marti lay on the floor sobbing, while Anna dressed and went into the younger children's rooms.

"Wake up, your father is dead. Wake up!" The youngest stood silently by her bed, confused: *Was this all a dream?* Norma, so totally confused now, didn't know what to feel.

Anna went into Alfredo Jr.'s room and found him crying on his bed.

"What happened to Papi?"

"He died... Get dressed. We are going to the hospital."

"Where is Mami?"

"She's getting dressed. Hurry."

Jimmy suggested that Anna stay home with the younger children. Marti would need to spend several hours making arrangements.

Jimmy held Marti tightly by his side as they entered the hospital room where Alfredo's body was being kept.

"He looks so tired," Marti said as she was led behind the curtains. She touched his cold face. "Why, he is just sleeping. He will open his eyes and smile. Please, Alfredo, wake up. Come back to us... I don't know what to do without you! Please wake up. This can't be happening... please wake up!" She was shocked by her urge to pull the covers back and climb into bed with Alfredo, so she could feel his arms around her. She fell into Jimmy's arms and wept for a long time. He had no words, only crying softly and holding her close.

"We'll help take care of you and the children. I am so sorry," Jimmy kept repeating in soft Italian as though singing a lullaby.

Shaking his head, Dr. Shapiro looked over to Alfredo.

"His heart, even at thirty-nine, was so enlarged. I'm surprised he lived this long. His left valve leading out of the heart was very damaged. It grew even more enlarged trying to pump the blood, which regurgitated back into the heart rather than leave it."

"Wasn't there something that could've been done?" Marti managed to ask through her tears.

"There is no successful open heart surgery yet. That is what he needed, a valve repair or replacement."

"Not here, maybe in the large hospitals?"

"No, even in the City hospitals. They do not do open heart surgeries yet. Maybe in the future."

They all came to the funeral in the Grand Street stone mansion with a view of the Hudson River: Mr. And Mrs. Rivas, Alfredo's brothers and sisters, Lola and her Carlos, neighbors, and other friends from the City. Flowers suffused the casket. Junior and Norma, left unsupervised, were pushing each other in a wheelchair that they found in the hallway, anything to avoid seeing their father's body. Marti found them and pulled them next to the coffin, where they stood for a long time until Marti forced them to kneel so they had to face their father.

Norma looked first at her father's hands. They used to open and hand her packs of Juicy Fruit gum when he returned weekly from the City. Her eyes traveled up the gray pinstriped suit sleeve to his chest. So quiet now. His tie looked a little crooked, but she dare not touch it. Her mother was standing next to her and would inflict a quick blow if she did.

His eyes were closed...a slight grin, body straight. She wanted to ask that he come outside while she climbed a tree and hung on a branch, to show how strong she was, telling him of her week's activities: *I visited Uncle Juan, who took me to feed the pigs with our food wastes. They gobbled it, Papa. I missed the school bus once and Uncle Tony drove fast until we caught up with it. I went ice-skating at the Grimm's pond ... I didn't fall ... only a few times, really. Ginger had her kittens in the corner of the barn ... you know, where the hay is piled. Mami said we could visit Anna in the City when you come home from the hospital.*

She wanted to touch his cheek, to wake him up like she did on Saturdays to feed the chickens together.

"Kiss his cheek," whispered Marti. Realizing that they could not reach him, she bent down and kissed his cold face. The children stood completely still. As soon as they sat, people started to come by, all whispering things like, "If there is something we can do, just ask..." Norma would remember her mother later saying that the worst part was seeing those visits dwindle as time went on.

The sky, on this barely above thirty-two-degree day resembled sherbet: a layer of dark violet, then deep orange, then a strip of violet again as the sun set. The guests had left. Several days had disappeared. Anna and Jimmy sat in the kitchen drinking café con leche with Marti, who watched the children playing outside in their snowsuits.

"Marti, we need to talk now."

"Discuss what?" Marti had slept through the night for the first time since Alfredo's death, but felt every muscle in her body ache.

"We need to discuss your future. Where will you live?"

"The house is done on Route 32, Jimmy. I'll move there as planned. I can sell the farm later."

"Do you mean that you intend to stay up here?" Anna immediately realized her mistake. She turned away, but tripped a little over the brass floor lamp.

"Yes, I mean here!"

"It will be hard for you without family."

"But I do have family. Evangelista and Juan are nearby. Besides, I have friends from the church."

"We understand that. How will you afford to live here?"

"I 've gone over this, Jimmy, ...I told you... I could make an upstairs apartment to rent in the new house, and get something in Newburgh."

"But you can't drive good enough!" Anna felt her face was aflame.

" I'm learning on the station wagon!"

"It is good that Alfredo purchased such a strong car!" Jimmy glanced up at the smiling women, pleased that he had chipped against their angry wall.

"There are many factories and stores here. I can embroider insignias like I did in New York."

Jimmy said, "The war is over. There will be fewer military hats."

"Oh, I can find something," And sure enough, Marti did. After learning to drive, she had applied for a job at the Orange County Coat Factory in Newburgh, misleading the manager into thinking she knew how to operate a factory sewing machine. Later, she would stay at the factory late into the night practicing.

"But a woman alone with three children!" said Anna.

"I have only two children at home. Maria will go to college soon."

"Anna, shook her head. Come now, you are a woman alone!"

"Well, *you* were a women alone with a child and did fine!" Anna sat down and smoothed down the creases of her housedress, glancing at Jimmy for help. She braced her body for what she feared might be said. Jimmy gave Marti an arrow-sharp look, shaking his head, as if saying,

"No, please....don't."

"You found a job hardly knowing English." Marti went on, carefully choosing her words. "You found a husband.... bought a brownstones. *You have shown me that anything is possible if you work hard,* Marti thought to herself, now mature enough to keep her feelings shelled this way, but then thought...

"And lied to everyone about 'your niece' so everyone considered you respectable. At least I married!"

Anna stared straight ahead. Tears came, as she thought, *you will survive this. Despite those Oblate Sisters who put five-hundred-year-old ideas in your head, but they did teach you many skills.*

"Good then, yes." But Anna still held in bitter feelings.

Even among them... those nuns... there were those who gave birth out of wedlock, thought Anna, now also shelling her true feelings into a box. It was of no use with such an opinionated woman. This box decorated with life's filigree, closed...sealed. Yet the seams leaked intermittently, unable to contain the substance within.

"You want more coffee, *Viejo?*" Marti asked Jimmy. "I'm not going back to the City to live in your house. I am a grown woman and can take care of myself. It is the fifties, not 1922. Many women live alone with their children. Look at all the widows from the war!"

Anna nodded, tears streaming.

Epilogue

When the waters became calmer, Marti accepted the opinions that the farm should be sold as soon as possible. She used some of the insurance money to have a rental apartment built in her new house.

Marti did eventually learn to drive as she promised. She drove in spite of the perpetual sound of honking that came from the cars driving behind her, and the frequent requests from police to pull over as a result of illegal traffic maneuvers.

Anna and Jimmy would visit on the weekends and help with the children. Tony retired. He and Beatrice moved into a bungalow on Juan and Evangelista's farm.

The lemon-colored farmhouse stood empty like a haunted house in a movie. Marti walked to the tree and sat on the circular bench built by Alfredo. She studied the fabric of her housedress, noticing a rip next to a pocket. *Got to sew that,* she thought. The horn sounded as nine-year-old Alfredo Jr. slid against it, wrestling with seven-year-old Norma. Marti stood up and looked over to the worn fence Alfredo and Tony had built, feeling it was a miracle that it stood up to the cold winters. She then made her way toward the parked car.

Years later Alfredo, Jr. had come to finally learn the truth about his mother---and hers. In the long journey of his family, it was one of many truths, seen from sides of shade and light. Like a maturing field...

Colado

ABOUT THE AUTHOR

I recently completed the novel "Anna and Marti." It is based on my Cuban family and their experiences living in the U.S., including Tampa, NYC, and the Hudson Valley.

I am a retired teacher, who began writing letters and opinion pieces in local and professional journals in order to complain. These experiences led to taking journalism, photojournalism and creative writing classes at Empire State, Lehman, and the New School Colleges. I have writing credits in a variety of publications, including the Poughkeepsie Journal, Hudson Valley Times Herald Record, Beacon Sloop Club "Broadside", Brooklyn "Caribbean Life Newspaper," Lehman College-"Meridian," and the New Paltz, N.Y. Caribbean and Latin American Support Project - "CLASP" Newsletter.

My husband, cat, and I spend time with family and friends between homes in upstate New York and the Bronx.

"Carry your spirit during your travels and lighten your load with humor. It makes the struggles bearable and brings smiles within to one's lips."

"I am a sincere women from the land where palm trees grow, and I want, before I die, to provide my soul's versos to bestow."
Inspired by: Jose Marti's "Versos"

157

Colado

158

Look for Colado's upcoming project:

"Writing the Metro North"
A collection of short stories relating to various experiences
of riding the Metro North while commuting from the Hudson Valley
to New York City.

For more information and updates please visit:
www.coladowrites.com